I0745480

CASTAWAY STRANGERS

Castaway Strangers

Written by
Starr Green

Earthy Info
Corvallis, Oregon

First edition November 2021

Cover art and map by Megan Scott
Cover design by Eathy Info
Interior book design by Earthy Info

ISBN 978-1-955561-02-0 (softcover)
ISBN 978-1-955561-03-7 (ebook)

Library of Congress Control Number: 2021941285

Earthy Info
Corvallis, Oregon
www.earthyinfo.com

MAP

Silver
Tides
Blue
Valley
Bay
Main
Camp
Shuttle
Drop
Cove
Salt
Cove
Headland

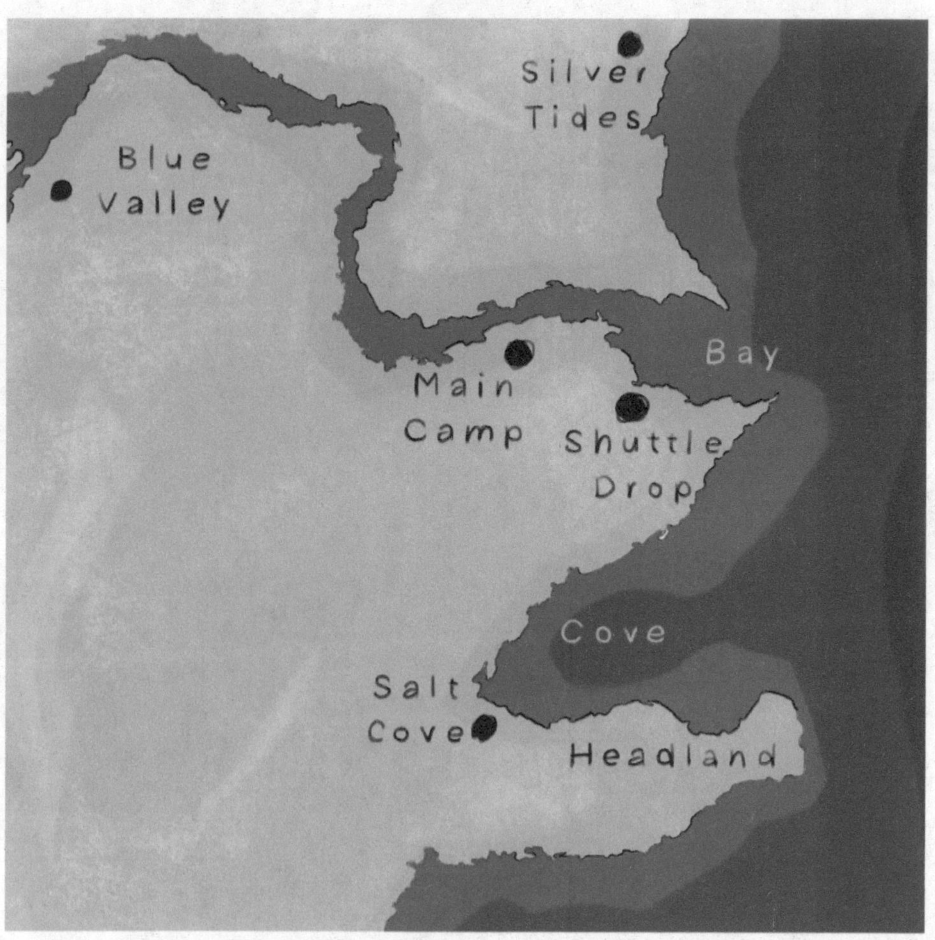

Table of Contents

CASTAWAY STRANGERS
MAP
PROLOGUE
CHAPTER 1
CHAPTER 2
CHAPTER 3
CHAPTER 4
CHAPTER 5
CHAPTER 6
CHAPTER 7
CHAPTER 8
CHAPTER 9
CHAPTER 10
CHAPTER 11
CHAPTER 12
CHAPTER 13
CHAPTER 14
CHAPTER 15
CHAPTER 16
CHAPTER 17
CHAPTER 18
CHAPTER 19
CHAPTER 20
CHAPTER 21
CHAPTER 22
EPILOGUE
Sneak Peek!

PROLOGUE

Finn

White. Floors, ceiling, walls. All white. Worse, the front door behind him was gone.

"Where are we?" Finn tried to keep the worry from his voice.

"My home." Helena, the girl he'd followed from the school cafeteria, walked away, leaving him with nothing to do except follow.

As they approached the far wall, a doorway shimmered open.

In a split-second decision, Finn ran back to where they had come through, hoping it would open back onto the street, but the shimmering didn't happen.

Helena waited patiently. "The airlock door does not open automatically. That would be poor design. Come."

Following Helena as the only way to gather more data on his situation, he tried to push away a panic attack.

The floor started to vibrate.

"We are nearly to your quarters. When you get there, I suggest you strap in." As she finished giving the instructions, a new door shimmered open, showing a reassuringly familiar bed, chair, and sink in a small room.

Helena sat on the edge of the bed as Finn strapped himself into the chair's attached seat belts. "You have some buttons there on the seat. You are welcome to try them out."

"Why am I here? What do you want with me?" He demanded.

"You are going to Aeymay. Good luck with your new life Finn."

He watched Helena disappear as the door shut. If Helena was her real name. As soon as they had arrived here, she appeared nothing like the teen girl offering to show him a new classroom by the high school field. Her jeans and tee shirt now replaced by a white jumpsuit. Her previously amber skin was suddenly blue-tinged.

He pressed the first button on the armchair, and it swiveled away from the door to face the wall. He did not understand what use that would be until he pressed the second button. The wall rolled upward, revealing a window running the length of the room, floor to ceiling. The view was of a slowly retreating Earth as seen from space.

"I knew it." He didn't want to believe it, but he had put two and two together, and his worries were justified.

CHAPTER 1

Olivia

Olivia watched helplessly as the unknown girl gasped for more air, fever bright eyes darting wildly without focusing. Her forehead covered in sweat.

"Help," she gasped, one last time and stopped breathing.

Olivia wondered if this was how she'd die too. Killed by something on this alien planet she was coming to love.

"The berries found with her were carefully scooped with a large leaf as a precaution for even touching them," said the short balding botanist.

He placed them gently in a row of other berries resting on big plate-sized leaves. "These have already proved either sickening or deadly. With paper now available, do you think you can sketch them realistically with just a charred stick?"

"I can try." Olivia examined the thick bumpy yellow squares. An odd paper for an even stranger ink - a mug of cooled dark brown tea - with a paintbrush of bound human hair.

The ingenuity amazed her.

After a week on Aeymay, she still didn't know where she fit in among these strangers, this large group of kidnapped castaways.

Some people here could build houses with mud, and she was holding paper made from plant pulp. She realized her comfortable life up to this point and had not prepared her for the future she was currently facing.

Pulling herself together, she decided her new goals in life would include being more useful. To do her part in this new civilization and make a difference here.

Getting started on the plant drawings, she asked, "Why are people eating the plants before they are approved?"

"You have not been tempted by all the unknown fruits in our tropical paradise?"

Olivia shuddered. "Not even a little."

"You must still have your food bars," he said. "Keep an eye on those. Looting is beginning. The less honest are taking easy food rather than risk the forest."

Olivia thought of her backpack, still half full of food bars, sitting in her unguarded doorless little tent, both provided by her alien abductors before being dumped on this planet.

The tent was little more than a tarp with poles and came with a thin mat to keep from sleeping straight in the dirt. Hopefully, her gear was doing okay without her for a moment.

"So, I'm drawing deadly food? Shouldn't we draw food people can eat?"

"The forest has plenty of edible food. Unfortunately, it's these pesky few deadly ones mixed in causing Doc to lose patients. Some are only stomach complaints and rashes, but others?"

They were both careful not to look in the direction of the dead girl. The botanist had nothing to cover her with, so he had left her on Doc's side of the grass hut, retreating to work near Olivia.

"I've been put in charge of food, and I'm desperately trying to catalog our surroundings into edible or poisonous. Your drawings will be a huge help."

"I'm leaving the sketches flat to dry. It would be best if they are not moved for a few hours." Remembering to put her happy expression on, Oliva asked brightly, "Is there anything else I can help with?"

"Yes, if you have the time."

"We all have too much time these days," said Olivia with her best laugh.

The botanist huffed. "I wish I had extra time. I'm only stopping to sleep."

A surge of incompetence washed over Olivia. Not only had she said the wrong thing, there were people here frantically working to help everyone while she'd been wandering around exploring for days. "What can I do?

How can I assist you?"

"If I had more people willing to forage, I could spend my time cataloging." He handed her a basket with a tall handle. "Can you gather fruits for me to test, with a few leaves from the same plant?"

"Right. I'm happy to help. Be back soon!"

"Of course, I don't have to remind you, but don't eat any of them."

"Right."

Coming out of the shade of the hastily assembled grass hut into the full sun, she thought again how her creamy skin was not evolved for this pounding heat. Her hazel eyes were not meant to view such a blazing bright light.

She was sweating through her shirt for the fourth time in a day. Although, survival would be much harder if everyone were shivering with cold rather than simply putting up with the heat.

Olivia was glad to take refuge in the thicker part of the forest. The dense tree cover allowed enough shade for a more tolerable heat. An irritating warmness rather than a sweltering physical pressure.

In the lush jungle, most of the trees had yellow trucks with various shades of orange leaves. Others resembled palm trees, with light blue leaves bleeding into indigo hues toward the center.

Woody and weedy vines in every color and shade climbed the branches while shrubs crowded around the bases. Edible-looking food hung on most plants, from tiny berries to dark blue coconut-sized fruits.

Bugs chirped, birds called, and lizards of all shapes and colors skittered along the ground or up the trucks.

In a city, this much noise and light mixed with so many smells would overwhelm her sensitivities. In the forest, she could enjoy the mixed soil and flower scents. The trees blocked the worst of the light. Even the repetitive animal sounds didn't bother her as much as traffic and machines.

People never understood why loud cars or flickering lights upset her. Growing up feeling so different from many of her classmates, she learned to hide the autistic quirks people didn't understand. Hiding always seemed the easier option than explaining it to people. Of course, the fewer people she spent time with, the longer she could go without explaining herself. Still, as always, those ideas were the opposite of her wish for friends.

A pleasant tenor voice broke through her thoughts, singing an old show tune, and a smile touched her lips. Around the next clump of trees, she found the owner of the voice yanking down rustling dried vines from branches high above.

His muscles strained and clearly visible since he was almost without clothing. Only a grass skirt tied around his waist provided him protection.

Olivia envied him. He looked more comfortable than she felt in her jeans and thick long sleeve shirt, even with the sleeves pushed up.

Everything about him was average. Neither tall nor short, with tanned olive skin. Hair and eyes a common brown.

In her brief pause at discovering him, she'd stopped directly under his workspace. In moments she found herself covered in dead leaves, flowers, and several lizards falling from the shaken treetops. The slow little creatures clung to her hair, sweater, and even her bare arms with tiny sticky fingers. She squeaked, resisting the impulse to shake them off.

His singing stopped mid-word when he saw her. "Oh, sorry! Here, let me help." Delicately tickling their fingers until the lizards unclasped, he placed them gently back on the tree.

"I'm Olivia." Staring pointedly at his attire with what she hoped was a friendly smile, she asked, "What's your job here at the camp?"

"Hello. I'm Finn. Currently assisting the clothing and basket team in finding more vines and grass. While trying out one of their creations." He swung his hips around in a tiny hula dance, the knee-length grasses swishing back and forth to show large leaves underneath them. "Nearly finished here."

This was more conversation than she'd planned to have with anyone today, and she'd already talked to the botanist a long time. More inane chattering was low on her list of priorities, but as she became aware of her own sweaty stench, she decided to distract him with the first thing that came to mind. "You are a great lizard handler."

"Thanks, I've had to remove them from the vines I gather. I hope these little guys don't need the dried vines we're removing."

"Ah." Olivia had no reply to that. Trying again, she said, "I'm assisting the botanist by finding new foods to try." She held up the basket as proof.

"It's one of the vine baskets I made." Finn smiled, seemingly pleased at its usefulness.

Olivia examined the basket, for the first time admiring what she held. It was obvious some effort went into the tight weave and striped two-color design. "Impressive work," she said, meaning it and feeling a little more comfortable with Finn.

"Thanks." He untangled the last lizard from her bunched sleeve and brushed some of the leaves off her shoulders and hair, asking, "Do you want to forage together? For a bit?"

She thought she'd done well not cringing away at his unasked-for touch. Would he make a good friend? Considering his offer, she finally asked, "Do I have to sing?"

He grinned. "Not unless the mood strikes you." Finn returned to his gathering, this time with less force. Trying to pull down one dead vine at a time rather than a handful. "Is there anything specific you are searching for?"

"Not really. The botanist said fruits."

"Maybe you can find something to make jam with," Finn said hopefully.

"Can you make jam?"

"No, I just like it." Finn grinned and shrugged.

Olivia both wanted to leave and keep talking to Finn. This was more interesting than most small talk so far. She was almost enjoying it. Completely forgetting about gathering and instead thinking hard for a new topic, she asked, "What did you want to do? As a job in your former life?"

"Former life?"

"It's what some people have been calling the past. It's like, we've all been reborn here. A chance to start over, to remake ourselves in this utopia."

"Utopia might be overstating it. I'll acknowledge the aliens picked a haven for humans, mostly, but I'd prefer Earth."

"What from Earth is better than here?" Olivia waved her hands at the bounty around them.

"Everything. The shopping malls, chilly mist-covered forests, whale watching, the pool I used for swimming."

She swung the basket back and forth, thinking out loud for an unguarded moment. "Oh yes, so much to miss. The useless crap in malls, the clear-cut forests, locating the few whales left, and artificially heating a whole building by burning limited resource fuel just to fool around in the water."

"I was not fooling around. I'm an athlete."

"Huh. Me too. I'm on a curling team."

"Was the training rink cooled with a limited resource fuel?"

Olivia grinned ruefully. "Fine. I suppose so."

Finn stopped pulling. The vines were forgotten. "My alien kidnapper told me we'll never leave here when they dropped us off. So, we must make this camp life temporary. We must have things to burn, things to eat, a safe place to sleep, a way to find comfort in this oppressive heat."

Olivia's jaw dropped. "Are you siding with one of the groups thinking we should try to recreate the past's broken civilization here on this planet?"

"Perhaps I am. I don't want to live as a peasant forever."

"Spoken like a rich spoiled brat."

Finn's charming smile twisted a little. "At least I'm a hardworking brat."

She mentally sighed and rolled her eyes, then shook her head. "I've got work to do. Good luck with your vine gathering."

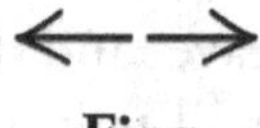

Finn

Finn dragged the dry vines behind him through the forest and back to camp. His hands full, his body working hard, and his mind entirely elsewhere. The argument with the auburn-haired girl was all he could think about.

The memory of her smiling eyes, probably at his rowdy singing, spoiled by the argument after. Olivia was probably never going to talk to him again. The vines caught on a bush, and Finn pulled violently, ripping several in half.

"Good grief. Those vines won't be of much use if they are shredded." The elderly voice behind him held amusement.

Dot, a self-described hippie who had nearly a lifetime of experience building houses from clay-based mud mixed with sand and straw. Something she was hoping to replicate here.

Finn took a deep breath before answering, releasing his anger at the frustrating conversion. Mostly.

"I guess I got carried away. Where are these vines headed, clothing or baskets?"

"Both if possible." Dot bent to untangle the vines from the offending bush, wincing from the added pressure on her knees, and grabbed an armful to assist Finn in carrying them.

Finn went pink, he should not need help from an over seventy-year-old to get these vines in, but he accepted the assistance graciously because he was growing fond of Dot.

"Good thing those aliens brought in a few of us old folk to provide, uh, let's see what did they tell me? Ah, a group of sensible elders."

Dot was one of the elderly who helped with leadership here, and she held the view that this planet should not be stripped like their last home. He was coming around to her point of view while also wondering if there was a middle ground they could take. Maybe not totally strip the land, but still live comfortably?

Dot dropped her vines as soon as they reached the meadow everyone was camping in, adding, "The woody trailing parts of this plant are amazing. It's only been a few weeks, but I still can't believe we get to live here."

Finn smiled at Dot. "Your hope gives me hope."

The image of Olivia floated into his mind. This world might have a few good points.

Still, he could not deny how wild his new surroundings were. What if another civilization was the only answer to feeling safe? Raised in a small coastal town, Finn had enjoyed everything a modern life provided. Books, microwaves, and hot showers.

He wondered if bathing in the nearby warm ocean would make him cleaner or salty. Either way, it was better than being sweaty. Probably.

Dot led the way into a grass hut, saying, "We have more vines for you, Dave. Skirts all round!"

Dave grunted recognition of the comment. A man of few words, the tough northern cattle rancher was unamused at being put in charge of the clothing production team, even if he was good at it.

"I should be out teaching survival skills or doing something more useful." Dave weaved a bit of sturdy grass into the waistband of a skirt, all the while glaring at it, like the skirt itself was responsible for his unhappiness.

"We've had this talk Dave, we don't need individuals surviving. We need group survival. Kids are falling over from heatstroke or running around the camp naked. Neither is good for morale. We need these clothes finished quickly."

They arranged the new vines into a tidy pile near Dave and left him to his work. On their way out, he said, "I'd rather go live alone than around these nature lovers."

Finn stiffened. Dave was a perfect example of everything that went wrong on the last planet with the wealthy in charge. He agreed with Dot on that point, at least.

Dot paused and pointed. "Our resident language guy is stressed today."

Finn noted the worry in Dot's voice. "Is there something for him to stress about?"

The language guy scratched something in loose dirt with a stick, roughly smoothed it with his hand, and tried again.

"I've offered him time off from camp chores until he's confident enough in the language of the native residents to hold a conversation."

"But, we haven't even seen the natives. Why the hurry?"

"The longer they don't come out to welcome us, the more likely it is they are hostile. So, knowing their language could be key to friendly ties when our cultures clash eventually."

Finn had heard the rumor that some people were told about natives. His escort had not been as chatty.

CHAPTER 2

Olivia

Olivia groaned as the message runner dashed away. She had promised Dot she'd assist in trying out the new fruit-gathering tool, but she had not known Finn was involved. She was hoping for Dot or at least a person she'd never met.

A new acquaintance was easy because social customs had all kinds of small talk set up for a new person. Also, people she'd spent a lot of time with were easy because they were already used to her.

Repeat meetings with possible friends were the worst. She could act social for a short time, but always missed an important reply or said something wrong. Often, she didn't even know what turned people against her.

Accepting that she could no longer hide in the crowd of a busy city, she was determined to make some friends. Eventually. Not with Finn, obviously. Planning out a few things to say and mostly vowing to stay quiet as much as possible, she followed the directions to arrive at the botanist's hut.

Finn was waiting for her. He didn't say anything, but she thought he seemed annoyed. She quickly filled the silence, saying cheerfully, "The message runner told me it's time to help with the new tool, so I'm here." She gestured at the stick Finn held.

He nodded and started toward the forest. Olivia's hope for continued silence was dashed one minute into the assigned task.

"So, you never said what you wanted to do. In your former life, as you called it." Finn glanced sideways at her. His tone was not angry or friendly.

Olivia wanted to run away, but pressed her lips together and stared at their target trees ahead. They were here for a specific task, so it was better to stay on topic. "How does the tool work?"

Swinging the stick around in one hand, Finn nearly hit her in the head. "Well, we've anchored a basket to the top of this smoothed driftwood. We're hoping to use it to shake loose those coconut-sized fruits. Currently, they are impossible for humans to reach, even climbing the tree. I've tried it out, but I can't both shake it loose and catch it. So, I was told there was a willing volunteer. You."

"Yep. Where do you want me to stand?"

Finn lowered the stick at Olivia like a lance, saying, "You are too far away, come closer. A little closer. Pretend you are catching something. Good! Let's try it for real."

He lined the basket up, lifted the stick high enough to touch the fruit with the basket, and gave the tree a firm shake.

Braced for her part, she cupped her hands and watched the stick swing toward her. Halfway through, she could tell the angle was wrong. She moved back, but not in time, so instead of getting hit with the pole, the fruit landed on her head, split into two pieces, and juice soaked her hair.

Finn rushed over. "Olivia! Are you okay? I'm so sorry. You were too close. I could not stop it from falling."

"Stop, stop. I'm fine." Olivia wiped her eyes with her shirt and wrung out the longer parts of her short hair.

The juice was only slightly sticky and smelled sweet. Actually, if this harvest went well, she might start washing her hair with it. She wouldn't tell Finn that though. She glared up at him. "Give me the fruit picker."

"It requires some strength to use."

She took the pole, lined it up with a fruit, and shook. With perfect aim, she dumped the fruit on Finn's head.

He was speechless as juice streamed down his chest and dripped from his hair. Then, he burst out laughing. "Only fair, I guess."

"I can throw forty-pound granite curling rocks with precision. I have enough upper body strength to shake a tree branch. I'll use the pole, and you'll catch the fruit."

"On it!"

Olivia lined up a second time and shook the tree. The large fruit landed in the basket with a satisfying thump, and she rolled it out of the lowered basket into Finn's waiting cupped hands. He placed it into a much larger basket he'd brought with him while she prepared the next fruit.

Again.

Shake. Drop. Catch.

The focus required halted conversation, and they fell into a rhythm.

Shake. Drop. Catch.

Repeat.

Moving in tune with each other. Olivia trusting Finn would be in place. Finn trusting Olivia would have the next fruit aligned for his waiting hands.

Shake. Drop. Catch.

Repeat.

Olivia's hyperfocus aimed at only the fruit and Finn.

As she watched Finn catch and place the latest fruit, she glimpsed what was behind him. She wanted to call a warning, but there was no time.

Leaning back slightly, she pushed the basket at his chest with all her strength. Caught completely off guard, he stumbled backward, barely out of range of the danger.

"Olivia!" His outrage that she would hurt him on purpose confused Olivia. Not because he felt it, but that she cared what he thought.

She pointed, and he finally saw his danger.

A plant stood at the base of one tree over, a thing out of a nightmare.

The above-ground roots of the chest-high plant had only three thick hairy stems, each topped with a giant flower. The long pointed indigo blue petals faded to an almost fluorescent purple in the middle of the flower.

Currently, the petals of the flowers closest to Finn were snapping open and closed. Four sharp thorns in the center of the flower clacking together like fangs.

Because the biting flower moved its long stalk at will, using the partly above-ground root system as a brace, it had come in range of Finn's ankle.

Finn, shaken from his push and fall, and then from seeing how close he was to getting bitten, pulled his legs to his chest and sat still for a moment to catch his breath.

Olivia shared what she knew, in case it was unknown to Finn. "The botanist calls them Biting Nettles. A couple of people have been brought in already dead after getting bitten."

"I've seen someone die in under ten minutes from contact with that plant. I've just been calling it the super scary plant. Thanks. For saving me."

With the plant still snapping toward Finn, its stalk was stretched out completely, exposing some berries bunching under the flower. A bird flew down, taking advantage of the plant's distraction, and snatched a berry.

"I didn't know it had berries," said Finn, finally getting to his feet and making his way back to Olivia. He eyed the length of the gathering stick, compared the reach of the long stems. "The bird ate the berries. Do you think they are edible for us too?"

"With so much other food, why bother the scary plant for a few berries?"

"They could be tasty."

Carefully staying out of reach, he swung the pole like a bat, smacking the plant soundly across all three mustard-colored stalks. The flowers went wild, opening and snapping shut on empty air, while underneath them, Finn used the end of the pole to roll the fallen thumb-sized berries toward him.

Forgetting to use her overly-cheerful voice Olivia stood to the side, arms folded and eyes narrowed at his antics. "You are nuts."

Finn pulled a leaf off a vine he knew was safe and used it to pick up a berry. An odd lumpy mix of black and purple, with long curling strings coming out of the middle and lots of juice pockets similar to a blackberry.

Olivia wrinkled her nose at the new fruit. "I'm not eating those. They are hairy and look disgusting."

"Coward."

Olivia shook her head and picked up the big basket of harvested fruit. "You can call me a coward all you want. I want nothing to do with that plant."

Finn carefully stored the berries in a pouch he wore attached to his belt loop and grabbed the pole to follow Olivia. "The birds eat them," he repeated. "They must be good."

She remembered to smile as she said, "Do you eat everything birds eat? Should I dig up some worms?"

"If you think they are edible," he replied.

"Actually, I have better things to do. Dot officially put me in charge of meeting the shuttle and new group orientation."

"Nice. A promotion from fruit gatherer to a glorified camp counselor."

"I'm excited. I can help shape thinking. Give them hope about this new home."

"Well, if anyone can give new arrivals hope, it's you and Dot. The environmental warriors."

Olivia rolled her eyes. "I've never claimed the title warrior, but I'll take it as a compliment."

"Don't."

Despite his flippant comment, Olivia thought he'd meant it as a compliment. She was warming to Finn. Their time harvesting together blossomed in her mind and made her flush. She'd felt so connected to him. Why were they back to insults?

A tall bush shaking by the river pulled her out of her recent and unsettling memories. A seemingly three-legged figure separated from foliage, but before she could get too worked up, she saw a human head and two regular legs.

A boy holding a black stick at waist height.

"I have not seen that guy before. What is he doing?"

Finn shrugged. "He arrived yesterday. I can't remember his name. An odd boy. He was taken with his metal detector, and the aliens let him keep it."

"Is there even metal on this planet?"

"If there is, he's probably the only one who can find it."

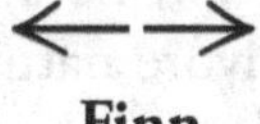

Finn

Finn burrowed deeper into the sand, finishing covering his legs, so just his upper body was visible. He'd built a tiny sandcastle, but when other people arrived on the beach, he quickly knocked it over. Acting like he was using the sand as comfort instead of a toy.

It was a beautiful day, and he had a good view of what he thought of as The Beach Lizards.

About two feet tall and three feet long, the large reptile-like beings skittered charmingly along the sand to splash into the waves. Some jumped into the ocean and did not return for a while.

Though it was difficult to tell them apart, it was possible. On some, the blue underbelly was darker, or the aqua stripe on their side was higher than others. Their orange leaf-shaped antenna also varied in size, and the orange fin along their tail could be longer or wider.

They all had the same shade of grey on top of their head and back and massive black claws.

He realized their blue underbelly matched the blue leaves in the trees. He knew he'd seen something in those trees. Their orange antenna mimicked the orange leaves on the low ground shrubs, so maybe they had hidden in those when he was near.

In fact, he'd bet those claws were for tree climbing and gathering fruit. If these herbivores were diving into the ocean, it must be safe for him too.

On impulse, he dusted much of the sand away from his legs, shed his grass skirt, and in boxers only splashed into the calm waves.

No stranger to saltwater, when he got about chest high, he waited for the current wave to pass, then ducked down in the water and opened his eyes.

The first sensation he noticed was the warmth of the water, comforting, enfolding him. As he let his eyes adjust, he saw the clear aqua surface water fading into teal closer to the gradually sloping bottom floor. When his eyes were wide enough, he caught motion.

The lizards! They were diving and curving around a school of graceful long-finned fish. The lizards appeared as nimble in an aquatic environment as they were comical on land.

Getting a deep lungful of air, he swam carefully toward the group. His earlier belief of their herbivore nature switched to his own omnivore attitude. In fact, he wondered how these fish tasted and if perhaps he could make a fishing line later.

He approached carefully, in case the lizards got into a feeding frenzy, similar to sharks. However, they didn't care about him, absorbed in their task. He swam with the lizards for a moment. In their same swirling pattern, keeping the school of fish in one big bunch and making them easier to pick off.

On swimming up for air, he saw one of the lizards had followed him. Farther than arm's length, but still close. At the surface, the lizard stared at him, its antenna shifting sideways and back, like a horse's ears at a strange noise.

Finn held still, a smile wrinkling his eyes. He was honored by this animal's gaze and still hoped it would not attack him. As if it could read his mind, the lizard's longer-than-usual antenna stopped shifting, and it ducked under the water, but immediately reappeared, and ducked again.

Finn ducked under the water with the lizard and watched as it started to swim back toward the fish. When Finn didn't follow, the lizard stopped and came back, then started again. The invitation was clear.

With a surge of joy, Finn followed his new friend back to the hunting. Taking a couple more breaks for air, he swam the swirling pattern with the lizards until they dispersed, leaving the remaining fish to flee into deeper water.

The long antenna lizard stayed by his side back to the beach. On arrival, Finn dropped to the sand, exhausted. The lizard approached, holding a whole fish partly in its mouth. The fish's fins pinned by long sharp teeth. The lizard stretched its neck out and dropped the still weakly struggling live fish into Finn's lap. Then sat next to him to stare out at the water.

It felt to Finn like his new friend was saying, "Good hunting, here's your part of today's catch."

For the moment, he was too tired to move, so he lay back in the soft sand, drowsing, letting sunny heat wash over him.

He woke to a familiar sound. The shuttle.

He sat up and saw Olivia standing nearby, ready to receive the newest residents.

She was watching him and asked, "Fall asleep mid-snack?"

Finn looked down at the dead fish, still in his lap, laughed, and shook his head.

He finger-combed his hair and slipped back into his grass skirt before everyone trooped down the shuttle ramp, blinking at the bright sunset.

Finn waved to them with the dead fish while Olivia announced, "Welcome. This is Aeymay, your beautiful new home. I'm your guide today."

A harsh voice from the crowd said, "Hey, you! The dishonest phony. Did the aliens hire you?"

Finn watched Olivia lose some of her confidence at the confusing statement and question. He didn't have to try hard to find the speaker. An old man in a navy business suit over a crisp painfully white shirt kicked through the sand in shiny black shoes. Pushing his way through the group, he came straight for Olivia and stood too close.

She frowned. "What? Paid? No. I'm like you. I've been here a couple weeks and it's really nice."

The man snorted. A strange mix of middle-aged and elderly. Chalky skin appeared baby soft. Gleaming bright white teeth didn't match his wrinkled lips. His orange tan didn't reach his eyes or ears. The dark hair seemed impossible for his age and must be dyed.

"I'm Jeff Phillips, so of course you've heard of me. I should be in charge here. I'm the best at organizing people."

Olivia smiled again, this time as reassuring as possible. "You just arrived, so let's get your whole group settled in together. You can meet some leaders later."

"Are you stupid? Get me settled in with the other leaders. It's where I belong." Jeff checked his watch, seemingly out of habit, then slowly lowered his arm, remembering time probably didn't matter here.

Finn pitied him. He remembered the initial disorientation of arriving. To aid Olivia and the newcomer, he stepped forward and said, "Whoa there, take it easy. Come along for now. We're going to get tents pitched, so you are comfortable tonight."

"I insist on an introduction to the failed leaders of this place." Jeff gestured around at the forest and the ocean, pausing to glare at the shuttle as it ascended back into space.

Finn clapped his hands. "First, we need to get everyone all sorted out. Tomorrow is soon enough for talking."

"I want a meeting with the losers in charge. Right now."

"Calm down," Olivia started to say, but Jeff cut her off.

"I'm a calm person. I'm always very calm. Believe me."

Finn held in a big sigh, reminding himself he was inadvertently part of the welcoming committee today. The first contact for the newest castaways and his tone would influence their mental wellbeing.

On the other hand, he was done with this guy. About to let the man have it, he paused when Olivia stepped forward.

Pointing to the headland, an hour's walk away, Olivia said, "Fine. Do you see the headland on the other side of the bay?"

Jeff shaded his eyes. "Yeah."

"If you walk along the bay and past a bunch of big lizards, you'll hit some proper sandy beach."

"Okay."

"Follow the beach until you get closer to the headland. The beach will start to curve to the left. Just keep going."

"That's where the leaders are?"

"Good luck." Olivia began herding the new group toward the edge of the forest where she could help them get their tents settled in Main Camp before nightfall.

"Wait!"

Finn saw Olivia roll her eyes before facing the most annoying person dropped off here so far. "What," she said.

"Stop standing there like a frozen slug, and take my bag." Jeff pointed to the tent pack he'd dropped in the sand.

"I can't," said Olivia, "all these other people are my responsibility."

"So, no one else is headed in my direction?"

"No one else asked to meet the leaders."

Jeff peered hesitantly toward the headland silhouetted in the gathering dark and reluctantly grasped his alien-provided backpack.

When Jeff was out of earshot behind them and the new group far enough ahead, Finn leaned over and said, "What a lie! Ruthless."

"Oh! Really? I guess it was mean, but I didn't lie. I never said the leaders were over there. I just told him he should walk away."

"Probably a bad idea, to send an old man off in the dark alone."

CHAPTER 3

Finn

"Meeting! Meeting now!" The message runner, finished with the short message, and ran on to the next group of tents to continue spreading the news.

Not for the first time, Finn marveled at the forethought of the aliens to make sure the first few groups came from countries speaking the same language. Getting started here would be challenging if they were also dealing with many languages.

Speaking of language. "Hi! My name is Finn." He plopped down in the dirt next to the translator. Finn had watched the boy concentrating on tracing symbols on the ground. He had been trying to find a natural way to introduce himself without simply interrupting the work. "You're learning the native language?"

"Well, I'm trying. My name is Scott." He held out a sunburned hand covered in freckles, and Finn shook it, looking into moss green eyes surrounded by a lighter sprinkle of more freckles. Scott's unbound, wavy honey brown hair framed his cheeks and flowed to his shoulders.

"I've been thinking about learning it too," said Finn. "Are you a language expert?"

"The aliens took me after a foreign language class and gave me the guidebook. They probably should have taken the professor instead. Have you noticed, we don't have any middle-aged people?"

Finn surveyed the crowd arriving around them. Roughly a hundred or so young adults, and ten more arriving every other day. All his age, or within a few years of it.

"Except for the really old," Scott continued. "As far as I can tell from asking around, the aliens are only raiding high schools and senior centers."

The elder women all stood tall, gathered at the front of the large open space designated as a meeting place and sports field. A few older men stood glumly nearby, off to the side. In a third group, at the front stood several younger people, including an openly nervous Olivia.

Dot stepped forward. An elder he admired more each day. Finn had been at her welcoming party when she got off the shuttle, and since then, she had proved a caring and clever coordinator.

"Hello, all! Past meetings have been about what the next focus is for our survival. This meeting is a little different. Today we are presenting you with several people. They are each going to speak for a few minutes on their vision for this community. Keep in mind we must pick a direction to all work toward. Divided we fall."

The first speaker was an old man outlining a rough idea for a single town containing all the people. Those with skills could set up shop and take in the unskilled. Then a barter system could be set up. Those with the shops would be in charge of feeding the workers after the set amount of work was finished each day. No work equals no food.

Finn thought this sounded a bit medieval. So easily could some people rise to power while others remained poor laborers. Who would be rich and who would be poor?

A young boy came forward, and several other older boys stood with him. The designated spokesperson explained how there was nothing wrong with civilization. We need to get back to it as soon as possible. Much as the man had done, he outlined a single city with jobs. It resembled what everyone had known in Earth's current civilization. A money system with paying jobs, some paying more than others according to skill.

Finn frowned. This was the idea he'd privately signed on to support. However, explained directly after the last idea, he could see how this also contributed to the rich getting richer and the unlucky staying poor. So, again, who would be rich and who would be poor?

A voice from the crowd, loud and tinged with anger, announced, "It's my turn to speak."

Dot shook her head. "Good grief, Jeff. Your plan is not fully formed and was already turned down for this meeting. If you have more of an idea, please come talk to us after this meeting, and perhaps you can speak at the next one."

Finn watched the businessman's face go red. "Everyone calls me a genius. I deserve to be heard."

Dot cleared her throat, drawing attention back to herself. Addressing the crowd as if there had been no interruption. "Keep in mind, if we are going to succeed, we'll all have to compromise and work together. We need a unified vision to work toward. Finally, it's time to hear from our last speaker, Olivia."

Despite the sweat on her forehead and clenched jaw, when she took Dot's spot at the front, Olivia's voice was joyful, yet urgent.

"Thank you, Dot. I agree we must work toward a common goal, and that goal should be the protection of the land we are living on. Earth was destroyed by greed, and we can't allow it to happen here."

She held up her hand, showing one of the slow lizards perched on her fingers.

"I propose a community living lightly on the land. With the land. We can build mud huts and seasonal grass huts among the trees without harming them. We would be in small family groups, tribes, but connected to each other for say festivals or larger food gatherings."

Olivia paused, letting the chatter of the crowd die down.

"Living much as we are now, working together toward a continued common goal of surviving. How wonderful it is to not have a job, working under a boss for someone else's profit. To instead, finish your community work for the day and have plenty of free time. Everyone has enjoyed how bright the stars are here, how clean the air, how unspoiled the meadows. Let us leave the beautiful world just as it is, live with it, be a part of it. Thank you."

Finn tried not to show any outward sign of his interest in this idealism and strange way of life. He had already pledged to support the money town. He leaned over to his new friend and said, "She's over-enthusiastic."

"Well, she's right," said Scott.

Suspecting a potential ally for Olivia, he asked, "You don't think her ideas are too much? Sounds like a hard way to live, always just barely surviving."

"It depends on how it's done. It could take more work, so that's a worry. I also think it would provide meaning to life. Maybe more free time. Anyway, it's worth looking into."

Picking apart Olivia's ideas, they didn't sound too bad, actually. Did he want to help build a city just to take a job in a store or office? The alternative, though. Living as part of a tribe, one member of a working whole in a moneyless society. It sounded like a mess and perfection.

Despite Olivia's assumptions, he loved nature. Admittedly, he often chose not to watch what was happening to it from his unsustainable lifestyle. Yet, it didn't mean he hadn't mourned its demise.

This speech had shaken his understanding of how communities worked. Could Olivia's idea be possible? Either way, her eager energy was contagious. Maybe, he could keep an open mind. Try to see the best in this new world. Until proven wrong.

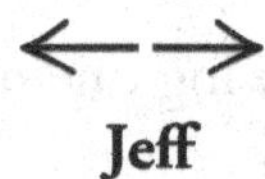

Jeff

Jeffery Phillips the Third glared at the youth going on about the environment and not harming it. The same childish girl that sabotaged his arrival, sending him to the middle of nowhere when he'd first arrived.

By the time he returned from the red herring and found the camp, it was full dark. He had no hope of setting up his tent and had to sleep out in the open.

Waking partly in the mud ruined both his suit and his image when presented to the other elders. None of them took him seriously. All those women acting more important than him.

All his troubles so far were either this girl's fault or the other self-appointed leaders.

Jeff scowled. The girl's idea to live in tribes? Barbaric.

Before the meeting started, he'd talked to the crowd, learning the people's thoughts on current rules set by the so-called Elders. Most people in the crowd wanted to kill the local animals for food, and only a few were worried about ruining the forest.

Jeff didn't have an opinion either way. As long as it would put him on top, he'd say whatever these fools wanted to hear.

So, if he was in a leadership position, he'd let the crowd hunt. This would get most of them on his side. The kind of support needed to stay in power.

"Thank you, everyone. Let's all consider what we've heard here today, and we'll meet again soon. Blessed be." Dot gave a cheery wave as the crowd dispersed.

Jeff seethed. That should be his role, the leader of the leaders. It's the role he was born for and always held, even in grade school.

The crowd was rushing toward the new clothing hut, and lost in thought, he got pushed toward it. He might as well visit. His clothes were damaged.

A clerk came up to him, a man about his age. "Everyone is allowed two items. Choose carefully. Let me know if you have questions."

"Why are you in here? Doing the job of a teenager instead of with the Elders?" So far, Jeff had not seen many older people, and only women on the council.

"Apparently, they don't want me, and if you are asking, then those nature-loving free thinkers didn't want you either. Hi. I'm Dave Coleman."

Jeff shook the offered hand, noting the customer service tone had left Dave's voice, replaced with the same bitter anger boiling through his own brain.

"Yeah, they missed out on having me lead them. It's a man's job, and those women are having tremendous problems running this place. Believe me." Jeff let out a deep sigh. "Why didn't they want our great talents?"

"For myself, I don't agree with the uncivilized pagan outlook they all want to force onto this community. Probably because we are men."

Jeff saw the utility belt worn over Dave's grass skirt. A fire starter and a knife both visible. He took a leap. "One hunter to another, I can't believe they are not allowing us to eat better by using the forest fully."

"Exactly!" The veins in Dave's head stood out.

Jeff knew he'd hit a nerve. "If it stays up to them, we'll never eat meat again. Ever. How do they get to make the new rules if we're way better?"

"Exactly!"

Jeff smiled reassuringly while internally cheering. Dave was putty in his hands. "Those phony leaders could hear us in this doorway. Let's move over there."

Dave nodded at Jeff's suggestion and led them to the back corner. Holding a grass skirt at chest level, he shook it. "Look at these things I was forced to make. Primitive. I'm sure we could create something better if I was allowed to skin and tan the reptiles here."

"Yeah." Jeff's agreement spurred the tirade on.

"And look at this! This mud, cleaned and dried into balls. They say it's to rewet and spread over our skin, apparently to protect against sunburns. Like, if we rub ourselves all over in mud like a savage, they hope we'll think like one."

Jeff had a little bit of trouble following the logic, but nodded encouragingly.

"I ran several large ranches. I know how to lead," continued Dave. "We must have real leaders in charge. Competent people ready to build a government and economy."

Jeff nodded again. "Of course, I started as a leader of several banks before going on to bigger things, but I'm the best at running things. You are a great leader, like me. You shouldn't be working in this dump."

"The current system benefits all the lazy people," said Dave.

"They are eating the food and wearing the clothing you worked hard to make, and what are they contributing? These leeches must be harnessed to the workforce and earn what they use."

"Exactly!"

"Dave, like I said, you don't belong here. What if we start our own group? They have declared themselves leaders. We can do the same."

A light lit in Dave's eyes. "Exactly."

Hooked.

Jeff grinned. Now he had an assistant, so taking over would be much smoother. He'd have to remember to treat his new employee as an equal, but it shouldn't be a problem. "What's the plan?"

"Leadership Necklaces." Dave pointed across the hut. On one wall hung a dozen necklaces made of a woody vine with bright leaves and feathers woven on them. "We just finished making them, so the people can tell who is in charge."

"Perfect. Let's go get us a couple." Jeff could not wait to wear this mark of honor.

"You go on ahead. I need to let a couple people know I'm leaving."

Jeff nodded and charged forward. He reached the necklaces with no issue. In fact, several people were admiring them, but when he removed one, a voice behind him objected.

A young girl came forward saying, "Sorry sir, those are only for leaders."

"I am a leader."

"I know all the leaders. I've never met you." Barely more than a preteen, the girl managed to pull off a stern glare usually seen on the older women he divorced.

"I am a leader." Jeff started to put the necklace over his head, and the girl yanked it down.

Another voice from behind him came to his aid. "He is a leader. On Earth, he runs his own company and has a huge yacht."

"I meant a leader here." She grasped the necklace firmly and ripped it from Jeff's grasp, damaging it in the process. Standing guard in front of the rest of the necklaces with arms folded, she glared at Jeff and his defender.

Jeff examined the strange boy who had spoken for him. Large brown eyes peered from under a full head of messy dark curls. His olive-skinned round face and visible arms were luminescent with youth and health. "Who are you?"

"Oh, hi! I'm Alan, the Ghost Hunter. I'm a big fan!"

"You should be. I'm a big fan of me too. Whatcha got there?" Jeff was usually able to maintain a friendly tone for his fans. However, he was still unsettled by the necklace confusion.

"Metal detector. I begged those aliens to let me keep it."

Alan launched into a story about his capture by the aliens. Jeff only listened to the beginning before nodding and following Dave out of the hut.

CHAPTER 4

Olivia

Olivia wanted to explore. Curious to know what was beyond the camp. Toward the south, a headland jutted out into the water. What was in the forest on the headland? What was beyond that?

She mentioned her plans for exploration to Dot, who insisted she take someone with her. Suggesting the language guy who needed a study break.

Wishing she'd just gone without telling anyone, like her usual crazy plans, she pushed down the dread of having to talk to someone unknown for two days. Maybe it would be fine.

"Thanks for coming with me," said Olivia as they broke a new trail together.

"No trouble," said Scott.

"Although, I don't understand why you brought him." Olivia glanced back at Finn, trudging along a few feet behind them.

"Well, exploring is worrying, so I thought we should bring along one more person. Anything can happen out in nature."

"I suppose so." Olivia was surprised it was so easy to talk to Scott. His pace in both speech and walking was easy to follow.

"Even though nature can be dangerous, I still love it, though," continued Scott. "I wish people were taking better care of the Earth."

"Right? I'd been thinking of getting a career in environmental politics. I had so many ideas and plans to save Earth," said Olivia.

Scott's shoulders drooped. "Earth is too far gone to save, at least as a place for humans to live."

"What? Why?"

"Uh, it's something I was told once."

"Hopefully, it's not true. I dream our families have been able to move on from our disappearance. Eventually, humans will find a way to halt the destruction of Earth."

"Seems unlikely."

"A moment ago, you said you loved nature and the Earth."

"I do. It's just, well, anyway. Are you always so cheerful?"

"I try to be!"

Olivia was saved from further reply when the trees parted. The stretch of empty flat high ground they were standing on gave them a view of the cove in the distance, created by the headland.

"Gorgeous," said Olivia.

"At least it's a good place to camp for the night," said Scott.

"Actually, it would be a great place to live," added Finn, finally catching up just in time to hear Scott's last comment. "Has anyone named the cove yet?"

Scott frowned. "I wonder if the natives have a name for it?"

She listened with half an ear while the boys chatted, but mostly Olivia's attention was on the space they found. Naturally high and open, but with a few large trees for shade. A breeze brought the scent of the ocean nearby, but not close enough to worry about possible high tides. Enchanted by her favorite place so far, she said, "How about Salt Cove? For the name."

Finn smiled at her when she briefly looked at him for his opinion. "I like it!"

Scott glanced again at the view and around the open space. "Yes," he finally agreed, "it fits. It's also a nice flat place to dance." Scott did a bit of fancy dancing footwork.

Olivia laughed and joined him with a few moves as well, saying, "Right? I can do that. I took lessons."

"Me too," Finn said as he joined in, adding some salsa steps. "I wonder how many of us here on Aeymay would want to attend a dance. Everything has been too stressful lately. We should throw a party."

"Sure, let's do it, it might be fun," said Scott.

Olivia shrugged. "I could take or leave a party, but I like dancing."

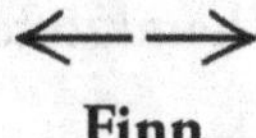

Finn

Finn inspected the party preparations with pride. A large bonfire burned merrily on a flat part of the bay. Above the wet sand, yet far from the trees. In the dusk, it was bright. In full dark, it would glow magnificently.

Not too close to the fire, new woven mats laid out in pairs marked where the speed friendship event would take place. On the other side, soft dried grasses had been scattered for a temporary dance floor.

He'd used his own tent tarp to layout the food baskets and arranged with the elders to serve as staff, so all the young people could participate in the gathering.

Attendees began arriving as the sun sunk lower into the horizon. Olivia appeared from the darkness of the trees. "All the preparations are so nice."

Finn detected sincerity in her usual unnaturally bright tone. "Thanks. I think it will be great. A good break from surviving."

In place of her jeans and sweater, she wore new clothes. A knee-length grass skirt tied low around her waist, with one of the women's chest coverings. A necklace with an excess of flowers secured in place by a single knotted tie around her upper back.

With his attention entirely on Olivia, Finn had not seen Scott arriving with her.

"I agree it looks nice. Hopefully, it goes well," said Scott. He also wore a new skirt, one of the ones with only long leaves and no grass. He bowed to Olivia, holding his hand high. "Would you like to dance?"

Finn's gut twisted at watching Olivia leave with her hand in Scott's. He identified his reaction as jealousy. Ridiculous. He told himself that didn't like Olivia.

Taking a moment to finish coordinating everyone into activities, he tried not to watch Scott twirl Olivia around to the beat of drums. Coming in close and then twisting away, only to get much too close again.

Finn started the first round of friendship speed dating and then sat next to the makeshift drums. Soaking in the pounding musical rhythm and heat from the fire. Watching Olivia match steps with Scott.

When the song ended, he jumped to his feet. The sudden impulse took him all the way to Olivia and Scott.

Scott, still holding Olivia's hand, offered it to Finn. "Your turn, if she wants to."

They both waited for Olivia to respond. Still out of breath from the last vigorous dance, she nodded, and the music started again.

Finn took both of her hands, and they began a dance similar to the one she'd danced with Scott.

He twirled them around and, letting go of one hand, moved the other to her bare back. The touch of skin on skin electric, but he had no time to savor it.

Matching her speed, he twirled her away a few steps, her grass skirt flaring out, only to come close again, body to body. Her arms around his neck, they moved together a moment before he pulled away a step, her fingers trailing along his bare shoulders.

Gripping her hand, he twirled himself and then her in a swift motion. Their feet pounding the grass and sand together in matching footwork.

His surroundings melted into a blur of light and sound. In tune with Olivia. This whirl of movement somehow also reminded him of the tree harvest they'd done together. Practically sensing what the other would do. Moving in perfect harmony.

He twirled her again, and she faced him. His hands on her bare stomach and his face nuzzling her neck.

The dance ended.

Finn wanted to say something clever, but he was out of breath. Also, for once, he was out of words.

Olivia stepped away from him, her short hair spiked in all directions, chest-covering flowers askew. Eyes bright and dazed. She breathed heavily another moment, then straightened. Pinning him with the usual bland look in her eyes, but overly chipper voice, she said, "Not bad!"

"What?"

"I mean, you managed well."

Finn held in his hurt. "Managed well? So, did you. I've danced with better partners, but you kept up." The untruth of this statement stung him as hard as it did her.

She opened her mouth, but closed it again. "At least I kept my hands to myself," she said, with a slight smile.

"Not that I remember. I felt your hands all over me."

Olivia narrowed her eyes and pushed him squarely in the chest. Finn held steady and laughed. "See, touching me again, just can't help yourself."

When she turned away, he let go of his anger at her reaction and asked quietly, "Are you going to run away again?"

"I never run away."

"You did when we first met. You agreed to forage together, but you took off."

Her body, which had been shifting away from him, swung back. With a big smile and a high-pitched voice, she said, "I'm not running away. I need a drink."

"Come with me." Grabbing one of the juicy tree fruits he'd pre-sliced into halves, they settled in front of the crackling fire.

"I can see why people don't like you." Finn surprised himself at his own honesty, but Olivia was irritating him again, and he could not figure out why.

"Who doesn't like me?"

"Half the camp, at least."

Olivia shrugged. "Huh."

Finn shrugged back. "It's said you rub people the wrong way. Also, that you keep them from hunting."

"That's Dot's plan."

"People are saying she favors your opinions on this topic. Because of what you presented at the meeting."

"We bond over the same values. That doesn't mean I'm influencing her. Besides, those rules were already in place when I arrived. How could I have been the cause?"

Finn drank the rest of his fruit juice and stretched out his legs in the sand. "Certain groups have decided to blame you, and it's hard to reason with people when they are scared."

"I don't understand people. This haven was given to us, and all we have to do is be careful with it to live here comfortably forever."

"I think our definitions of comfort are different."

Olivia set her drink down and wove her fingers together. "Perhaps. What does comfort mean to you?"

"I don't know. My soft bed. Tea in the morning. Family around me."

"You could have those things here. Eventually."

"It's not the same," said Finn. "Besides, we were not given this forest. We were dumped here."

"Why not make the best of it?"

Finn shook his head. "Why are you so hopeful all the time!"

"Why can't you be more hopeful?" Olivia asked.

"It's annoying. You're annoying."

"Well, why are you so gloomy all the time."

"I am not gloomy." Finn didn't think he was gloomy. Or, was he? At least, not as worried as Scott.

Olivia laughed. "Poor Mr. Gloomy, the spoiled brat of Aeymay."

"You apologize."

"No. You apologize." Olivia frowned, and it was the first time he'd seen her anything except cheerful.

"For what?"

"I'm not annoying." Olivia stated it without emotion or apology.

Fed up with the conversation, Finn stood and stormed away.

"This time, you are running away," Olivia called with a laugh.

Finn paused, but kept walking.

Olivia

Olivia forced her attention on the neanderthal in front of her. He was droning on about his hunting exploits. Yuk.

She didn't remember his name, or why she'd agreed to this speed dating. No, she knew. It was easier than avoiding Finn. Even with over a hundred people on this beach, he was everywhere.

She went over again what had happened after the dance. She'd told

Finn he did well, and she meant it. Then he said he'd danced with better people. She was not an expert dancer, but still, wasn't that rude of him? Or was she misreading the situation?

She had the same flow with him during the dance. The same as before in the forest, and he must have felt it too. Well, it didn't matter if Finn was nice to her or not. It's not as if she liked him.

The boy in front of her paused to let her reply, but she'd lost the thread of conversation. Quickly using some facts to change the topic, she said, "Look over there. We call them beach lizards. They live between the bay and the cove, but they come into the forests too."

The lizards were usually finished hunting by nightfall, but she realized it was still dusky as the group of them emerged from the water nearby.

"I've lived deep in the bush, killing and eating lizards and bats. I'll fit right in here." The irritating new guy pulled a large knife from his belt, and before Olivia realized his plan, he threw the knife toward the lizards, hitting one in the head. Instantly killing it.

"Got it! Now we have something to cook on the fire." He grinned at her.

Olivia's attention had never left the lizards, so she saw the flurry of action. Some smaller ones scattered, running for cover in the forest or diving back in the water. Others rushed forward. The largest one going straight for the knife thrower.

Olivia was dragged away by hands under armpits, pulled to safety into the crowd of humans. Glancing up, she saw Scott's grim expression and smiled thanks for his quick rescue.

Able to watch from a safe distance, she saw the knife thrower running away from the lizard. Without the knife, he was defenseless against a pursuer and scampered up a tree.

The chasing lizard didn't hesitate. Racing up the tree behind him, it snapped at the boy's ankles until it got a good hold on one, using powerful jaws to jerk him back to the ground.

The screaming started as soon as his ankle was caught. It didn't stop as the lizard dragged the boy through the dry sand. Then the wet sand. Finally, out into the soft waves.

A couple people tried to step forward, to help, but Finn held them back. Pointing at the line of lizards intently watching the humans, muscles bunched for action.

When the alien lizard reached deeper water, it dived, and the screaming cut off. Some tense moments later, only the lizard reappeared in view. Calmly gliding back to shore, with easy swishes of its powerful orange-finned tail.

Olivia hoped that would be the end of it, but the lizard came out of the water and, in a measured strides, moved directly toward the group of humans.

Finn stepped forward alone, separating himself from the group, and waving them to get back. He offered an open fruit by placing it on the ground and taking two steps back from it.

The lizard didn't even glance at the fruit. Staring at Finn an instant, then glaring around at the crowd, meeting a few eyes, making his anger known.

When the lizard started drawing in the sand with a claw, Scott pushed forward to translate.

"The writing says 'My name is Storm. Don't Kill Us.' It's written in the native language." Scott's shock vibrated through the silent crowd.

Storm glared at everyone again, his antennae flatted on his head, and stomped away, instead of the usual skittering.

After one more breath of stunned silence, the humans swarmed into activity. Some running back to camp, others rushing to friends, shouting about what happened.

Olivia stayed frozen, watching Finn and Scott confer grimly, too quietly for her to overhear.

CHAPTER 5

Finn

Two nights had passed since Finn watched one of the beach lizards kill a human. Everything was different now. Fear permeated the camp. So strong it felt like a physical object Finn could touch.

No one went near the beach or bay now, except Finn and Scott to escort Olivia to greet the shuttle.

Finn didn't think he was afraid of his friends. However, during his morning run through the camp, a wave of fear washed over him at each new person he passed. Until a new sensation caused him to stop abruptly in the middle of the path.

A boy walked toward him. His curly dark hair shining in the morning sunlight.

It was not the sight of the boy that stopped his running, but the feeling coming from him. Finn recognized two distinct emotions. His own confusion plus the boy's contentment.

The boy's mental serenity surrounded Finn's senses, like a warm hug. As he strolled past, the boy nodded and smiled.

"Wait!" Finn had not broken eye contact with him yet, so the boy waited with a cheerful smile. "I must know," said Finn, "aren't you afraid of the lizards?"

"Why would I be?"

"They killed a human."

"Self-defense. He attacked them first, and they didn't attack anyone else. So, why should I worry?"

"Ah, I see. True."

"Have a lovely morning!" One of the boy's large brown eyes winked at Finn as he nodded again and departed.

On the rest of his run, Finn focused on the emotions flowing through the camp. At each person he passed, he could feel their fear as before, but now, with his brain calmed, he could tell it was not his own fear.

Somehow, he was sensing their emotions.

He found Scott sitting by his tent, studying the translation guide while he waited for Finn. He reached out, on purpose this time, and sensed stress, in a troubled mind.

He plopped down next to Scott, settling into the dirt. Very little of the grass from this meadow remained after the humans trampled everything.

"What's wrong?" Finn asked.

"The fear in the camp worries me. Fearful humans do stupid things." Scott closed the book, but ruffled the corner over and over again, fanning the pages.

"What stupid things could they do?"

"Who knows? My main worry is they will group together and kill the Blue Kin."

"Who?"

"The lizards. Their name for themselves translates best as the-color-blue and not-quite-family, so I've dubbed them Blue Kin."

"I like the name, and I like the lizards too." Finn remembered the hunting party he'd joined and how they accepted him. "I don't want them dead."

"They are a sentient native species. It would not be fair to harm them after they let us live here."

"How do you know they let us live here?" Finn had not heard this tidbit before.

"The aliens gave me the translation guide and told me the natives agreed to let us stay on this planet."

Finn sat up quickly. "Did they also tell you why we are on this planet?"

"No."

Finn sensed something new from Scott, uncertainty mixed with something he could not place. How was he doing this? Always able to see another's point of view, he'd never before today been able to actually feel other people's emotions.

Finn was about to try to explain this to Scott, but hesitated. He'd sound crazy. "You've been waiting for me. Do you need something?"

"I just needed to talk about the Blue Kin. I tried to talk to Olivia. She seems not to care."

"Really?"

Scott ran his hand absently back and forth over a tiny patch of remaining grass next to Finn's tent. "Well, Olivia says the lizard's actions were defensive, but she's the only other person I've heard say it."

"I just met someone else who thinks the same way. He's the curly-haired guy with the metal detector. I think he was headed toward the river again."

"If we can gather everyone with this opinion, maybe we can band together and protect them. I don't want anyone hurt. Blue Kin or human."

"Me either." Finn agreed. Two killings were enough.

"Let me know if you find others. I'm going down to the river to talk with the guy you mentioned."

"Good luck."

Finn watched him leave, hope and determination radiating off of him like heat waves. He shook his head, clearing the other emotions away until only his own remained. Maybe he needed to go back to bed.

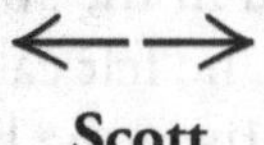

Scott

Scott knew things. He didn't want to tell the others, not with so much to deal with. What dangers lurked in the ocean beyond the waves? Or what dangers could be in the forest? Or even here in the camp?

Scared of never getting settled here, of all the plants killing them, and other fears lurking below a possible panic attack, if he thought about all their problems.

As usual, he didn't want to think about it, so he shoved the worries away. Into the same mental lockbox with all his other fears.

Now, the Blue Kin. Another problem for him to feel anxious about.

Across the river stood a boy scanning a rocky area with a machine at the end of a pole. "Hey! Metal Detector Guy!" called Scott.

The boy shaded his eyes with a hand to stare across the water. "Can I help you?"

"Hold on, I'll come to you." Scott lifted much of his skirt out of the way to cross the knee-high section of the river. He'd learned the new clothes didn't do well when wet.

On the last deep part, he gave up with lifting and gathered the whole skirt to hold it around his waist. The splashing water soaked his legs and the fabric of his underwear, but at least his skirt was saved.

When Scott finally scrambled up the slope, the boy said, "Nice view."

"What?" Scott glanced around at the forest and river. The view from here was nothing compared to others he'd seen on Aeymay.

"Nothing. I'm Alan. Unless you want to keep calling me Metal Detector Guy."

"Well, no. I'm Scott."

Alan smiled with an amused twist of his lips, a gentle crinkle to his brown eyes. "Can I help you with something?"

"Maybe. My friend said you hold a minority view on the lizards."

"Yes, I'm usually in the minority on a lot of things." Alan laughed, with a bit of sadness to it. "So, you're the language dude?"

All morning Scott had held in the swirling worry trying to overwhelm him. Standing here with Alan, he felt calm glide over him. "Yes, I've been learning to translate for the natives, the lizards. They're called Blue Kin."

Alan pointed to Scott's bare hands. "I usually see you with your little book everywhere you go."

Alan usually saw him? Had the boy been watching him? He'd never seen the other guy before. Although, getting a good look at him, it was surprising Alan had gone unnoticed by him so long. "I left the translation guide next to a tree before crossing the river. It's too valuable to chance on a river crossing, even at knee height." Scott, spellbound by Alan's gaze, became aware that he was rambling.

He often got lost in daydreams, but this time he was adrift in active conversation. What had they even been talking about? Oh, the lizards.

"Anyway, what do you think about the natives?"

"I don't think the Blue Kin should be feared if that's what you mean."

Scott smiled at the first instance of the name he'd created being used. "I agree with you. I'm afraid for them. I'm trying to find everyone who agrees, in case they need protection."

Alan shrugged. "I'm happy to speak for them. Although, they seemed pretty good at protecting themselves."

"Well, they don't know how awful humans are."

"Hey! I'm a human." Alan swung his arms wide, his eyes squinting into crescents as he laughed out loud.

"I know." Scott smiled back. Alan's contagious laughter caused him to smile wider and feel happier than he had since arriving on this planet. "You are human, but you seem calmer than most."

Alan nodded. "You too."

"Thanks."

"Well, let me know if you need help with the Blue Kin, or help with anything."

"Thanks," Scott repeated. As he crossed the river again, he wondered what else he could need Alan's help with.

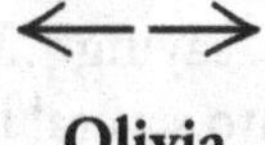

Olivia

"This is why we must live with the land, not against it!" Olivia's furious shout interrupted the tirade of an opposing force. A group wanting to gather what weapons they had and kill all the Blue Kin.

"Who put you in charge?"

Jeff's comment made Olivia's blood boil. "This is not about anyone in charge. It's about what's ethical. You can't massacre the Blue Kin. It would be murder."

"Those savage lizards killed a newcomer. They are a danger to everyone here. We have the chance to wipe them out. Let's take it!" shouted Dave.

A cheer went up from the crowd. More than half.

Scott's quiet, measured voice came from behind Olivia. "The Blue Kin are not a danger. Can't you recognize they only attack when provoked?"

"Who knows what will provoke them next?" Jeff raised a fist in the air. "Let's get them before they get us!"

"Yeah!" The crowd cheered louder this time.

Olivia despaired getting through to them. Fear in the camp had built the last few days, with hard feelings against the Blue Kin, but she had not believed Scott's worry would develop. Would humans rise up and decimate all other sentient beings? History repeating itself?"

"We must tread carefully here," Olivia's start of a new reasonable argument was cut off by loud laughter.

Dave pushed forward. "Romantic views about nature are for settled cities. Survival is what is needed here. Keep your sappy sentiments, and let us do what must be done."

Dot waded into the mob with her arms raised. "Everyone. Everyone! Please. Enough. Good grief. The elders have discussed some possibilities. Please reclaim your seats and attempt to listen again."

Jeff glared at Olivia, but sat down again with Dave. Olivia mirrored the action, as unwillingly.

"How stupid do you think these people are? Tell us what's really going on," Jeff shouted.

Dot ignored Jeff's outburst, saying, "We have more people now, so we believe everyone should split into several like-minded groups. These groups can start their own villages, with whatever values the group decides on. Perhaps one group can move inland, away from the danger of the lizards, and anyone scared can follow them."

Jeff shot to his feet. Still a commanding presence even with his shabby suit and his fake tan fading into a sunburn. "We should not have to run away. The smartest creatures should rule over the other creatures. How smart can those lizards be?"

"Yeah!" the crowd cheered.

Olivia's heart sank at the way this group was devolving into the worst behavior of humans. All her dreams of a fresh start for humanity evaporating like soap bubbles.

Dot tried to rein in the chatter again, but it was too late. Jeff had restarted the shouting, and the people would not be stopped.

Waffling between anger and despair, she backed away to the edge of the gathering, where she found Finn sitting alone.

Olivia snorted. "Can you believe this nonsense?" Taking a closer look, she realized Finn was not well, his eyes glazed and his head cradled in both hands. "Are you okay? Do you have a headache?"

"All the feelings," he whispered. "It's so overwhelming."

"They are unbelievable. I hope they do run away and make their own town. Then we won't have to deal with them anymore."

Finn sat a little straighter, focusing on Olivia. "It does sound like a good plan. To build a city far from the lizards."

"Not you too. You agree with them? How can you be afraid of the lizards? Just like everyone else."

Finn started to speak, but she'd had enough of stupid people. She weaved through the crush, heading toward the front. Dot would know what to do and how to make them accept logic.

Pain blossomed along Olivia's ribs. Someone had punched her. Hard. While she was bent over, someone kicked her, and she went down.

Finn

Finn's brain pounded with the tsunami of emotions raging around the hundred or more anxious people shoved together. He watched Olivia leave, wanting to explain he had been trying to agree with her. He didn't fear the lizards, only all these panicky people.

It was nice when she was standing by him. Using a new trick he'd learned, he linked his mind to her, which blocked out everyone else. Her frantic outrage mixed with despondent worry was still better than the waves of frightened anger coming off the mob.

He stayed connected to her, even as she stormed away, his mind stilled by even a brief exchange of words with her.

Suddenly Olivia's emotions erupted. Confusion. Pain. Agony.

Finn leaped to his feet, trying to find her. She'd disappeared. He could feel her near, but could not see her anywhere.

"Scott! Dot! Help!" He hoped one of them heard as he waded into the shifting crowd.

He almost lost his connection to Olivia twice, but new pain would flare in her mind, and he'd correct his path back toward her.

Finn found Olivia lying in the dirt, just as Dave was lining up a kick to her ribs. Finn threw himself on top of Olivia to protect her, his ribs receiving the pain meant for her.

The crowd joined in. Hesitant to inflict too much pain on a girl, but a male protector was fair game. Finn braced on the ground to rise, and someone stepped on his fingers. He screamed as one broke. Trying to scramble upright again, he was punched in the ear, and liquid started running down his neck.

"Enough! Enough!"

Dot's shouting seemed a far distance away. Finn was pushed from behind, and when he hit the ground a second time, someone kicked the other side of his ribs. Opening his eyes was a bad idea. Flashes of light shifted above him through the arms and legs attacking him. Someone kicked his thigh, a short boy reached down to punch his eye.

Just as he was wondering if he'd make it out of this riot alive, he saw the flash of a blade coming toward him. He recognized Dave's knife, but not the wielder.

The sharp steel sliced across his cheek, narrowly missing his eye.

The knife was coming back for a second swipe when something fell on him. He wanted to see what it was, but the knife coming straight for him was all he had attention for. Until he fainted.

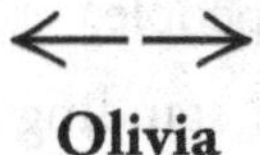

Olivia

Olivia, grateful for Finn's rescue, watched in horror as the attack switched to him with even more violence. She lost sight of him, but crawled on her fists and knees toward where she thought he'd fallen.

She threw herself on top of him, like he had done for her. Protecting him with her body. He was a mess, blood everywhere. She saw a knife way too close to his face and put out her hand to stop it.

The knife sliced across the back of her right hand, opening a long cut, but saving Finn's face from further damage. Someone stepped on her ankle, the sharp pain a slight distraction, but her attention was for the knife.

What was it with men and knives? First the lizard murderer and now this guy.

He was going for another strike when the boy's wrist was caught by Scott. The off-balance attacker dropped backward. Screaming as his supporters accidentally trampled him.

The press of bodies was too tight to carry Finn out, so Scott stood guard above while Olivia did what she could from below.

"Enough!" Dot's angry grandmother tone made a couple people pause in the fighting, which caused a couple of other people to wait. Olivia watched legs move away from her as the crowd separated, merging back into the smaller groups of people it had started with.

"Everyone! Go away and consider the new option of separate towns."

A newcomer, one of the oldest youths to arrive, leaned out of the money group and shook a fist at Dot. "Why? We'll be poor no matter what. This planet has no way to regain our former status. Instead of fighting each other, we should be fighting the aliens!"

A not unfamiliar idea. Olivia had heard this sentiment every few days as new arrivals always asked about it. The simple answer was no one was brave enough to try. Never had someone said it boldly at a meeting.

The newcomer stepped in between the groups, close to the front, almost taking Dot's place. "I say we attack the shuttle. Take control of it. Force them to take us home!"

The crowd with him roared agreement.

"Who is with me? Who will attack the aliens when they show their face tonight?"

The crowd with him roared again, this time with fists raised.

CHAPTER 6

Finn

Finn woke next to the river. Scott was untying his grass skirt, but when he started to tug on his boxers, Finn growled. "Leave it."

"I'm glad you are awake. I was getting worried." Scott smiled, but Finn could see the concern. "I'm going to float you in the river. It's colder than the ocean water. Maybe it will bring down the swelling and also clean you up a little."

"Can't be in the river it's against the rules." Finn could not catch a full breath and remembered the kick in the ribs.

"Dot said we could break the rules for this."

"No. I'm not in the mood for a swim."

Scott came into view again. "Your swelling is bad. If we can get some of it down, you'll heal faster."

"No. I think my ribs are broken."

"I'm certain of it. I thought we would get you cooled down and put you to bed."

"Second one skip the river. We have to set a good example."

Scott shook his head. "Well, it's your body."

"Yep." Finn tried a grin. It pulled on his injured cheek, and he stopped. "What happened?"

Scott let out a long gusty sigh. "Dot broke up the meeting, and you probably have a concussion. The people have decided to fight the aliens instead of the natives or each other. I wish they'd decided that before attacking Olivia for losing her temper. Who knew she had one? Anyway. Attacking the shuttle is a stupid idea, but it's got half the camp buzzing with hope for returning home."

Scott helped Finn sit up, and Finn accepted a cup of water to drink. "Aliens won't let it happen."

"I know that, and you know that, but the mob won't be swayed."

"When?"

"Today, if the shuttle keeps to schedule."

"It has so far. I want to go watch."

"You want to watch them all get killed? I guess it's one type of revenge."

"Not revenge."

"If you say so. If you won't get in the river, I'll bring the river to you. Hold here. We'll get you cleaned up and head to the beach."

Scott returned shortly with a soaking wet tee shirt and started to carefully wash away the blood.

"Mostly, I'm just bruised and broken. Only cut is on my face."

"It's not the only cut. Olivia's got a nasty one on the back of her hand."

"Olivia! They attacked her with the knife too?"

"Other way around. She tried to stop them, to save you."

Olivia had also come to his rescue? Last he remembered she was limp on the ground. Most of his brain fog was probably the concussion, but still, he could not wrap his head around this new revelation. He was sure she liked Scott and didn't like him at all. "You seem close to Olivia."

Scott grinned. "we're becoming good friends."

"Huh. Think you'll get together with her soon?"

"I'm not interested in her romantically."

"Why not? I mean me either." Finn trailed off, not sure what he'd meant to say.

"I'm not interested in any women."

"Ah." Finn took this in, too exhausted to ask for more details.

"You should go for it, though," added Scott.

"I don't think she likes me."

"Might be surprised."

Talking had taken all Finn's strength, and he lay back and accepted the kindness offered in getting him cleaned up. Any time he started to doze, Scott shook him awake, and finally, it was done.

The bruised muscle in his thigh made him limp, but Finn was otherwise mobile as they hurried to the beach. Arriving barely in time to watch the disaster play out.

"Let's go home!" The newcomer acting as leader, shouted when the shuttle was spotted. Boys and girls rushed forward, waving driftwood poles or the community's few knives.

Finn groaned. "Who gave them permission to use those knives?"

"I don't think this is the kind of group to ask permission." Scott helped Finn sit at the tree line. With a good view of where the shuttle landed, but well away from the action.

When the shuttle was in hearing distance, a few of the group backed away. Seeing them, others started to lower their weapons, rethinking their part in this dangerous plan. When several ran, many followed.

As the shuttle ramp descended, the leader became aware that only five boys stood around him now. "Cowards!" he shouted.

The remaining six shook fists at the retreating backs of their prior supporters as the shuttle settled. Once the new castaways were off the ramp, the ambush group attacked.

The battle ended quickly.

Six boys charged the ramp. Five died instantly by weapons pointed at them from the top of the ship. Seemingly drawn by their quick movements and firing automatically.

The leader, avoiding the motion-sensing guns, almost made it inside, but was pushed back by one of the aliens. A spear protruding from his chest, he fell from the top of the ramp, hitting the sand as the ship took off.

Finn shook his head, but wished he had not. The headache from before pounded to life again. He wanted to sleep.

His eyes were shut only a moment before Scott said, "Wake up, Finn. No sleeping for you today."

"I'm awake, but it's a near thing. I need a distraction. Talk to me."

"Is it bad, I hoped they would succeed?"

"Of course not. We'd all go home if we could."

"Hmm, home."

Finn opened his eyes at the odd note in Scott's voice and flare of misery in his emotions. His new friend's eyes glistened with unshed tears. Finn asked, "Are you okay?"

"Ignore me. Anyway, we're lucky to be here on Aeymay. We need to make the best of it."

"That's what Olivia's been saying the whole time."

Scott huffed out a small laugh and wiped his eyes. "Well, I know. It's just, today it sunk in for me."

"I think it's sinking in for a lot of people." Finn pointed to the group finally leaving the beach. Some were crying, and they all looked dejected. He didn't think it was the dead boys they cared about, having left the bodies where they fell.

Not willing to try himself, he had still hoped for their success, for a chance to return home.

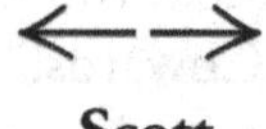

Scott

Scott sent Finn to Dot's tent alone, hoping he would be okay. Finn seemed lucid and mobile and should be fine on his own.

Scott didn't want to tell him that he planned to tend the six bodies on the beach. Finn would have insisted on helping, and he wasn't currently in shape for it.

Considering people in shape, his thoughts flowed to Alan. His strong arms, and bare chest, tapering down to, well, probably strong legs under the grass skirt.

As if thinking about the boy conjured him in real life, Alan walked onto the beach, rubbing the back of his neck and shaking his head at the dead.

Scott came up behind him. "It's a stupid waste of life."

Alan jumped. "Oh, you."

"I've been sitting at the tree line, wondering how to carry the bodies, and you appeared. Do you want to help me?"

"Alright." Alan waved around at the bleeding blank eyed-boys. "I would dig graves, but we don't have shovels."

Scott bent to close the eyes of the nearest boy. "There have been other dead, and there will be more, but we don't need to dig graves because the doc found a large deep hole, so he's been having the bodies dropped there."

"It doesn't seem respectful, but we can't leave them here. Head or feet?"

"Huh?"

Alan gestured at the body. "Are you carrying the head or the feet?"

"I'd rather do neither, but the strongest takes the head."

Alan grinned. "Guess that's you."

The first boy was relatively easy to lift and get to the deep sinkhole opening. By the sixth, Scott was sweating and breathing hard, his arm and leg muscles straining to keep up.

"This one is dragging a bit," Alan commented. His own breathing was also a little labored. "Do you want to stop for a break?"

"After. We're so close now. Unless you need one?"

"No. Let's finish."

As the last boy thudded into the bottom of the hole, Alan saluted, saying, "A good try, dudes. Rest in peace."

He moved away from the hole and laid on his back in a patch of grass. Scott followed. Both sprawled out, letting their breathing settle.

"Well, thanks for the help," said Scott.

Alan turned his head, his eyes finding Scott's. "I told you, you can ask me for help anytime."

"Oh, I guess you did offer that, sorry." Scott held Alan's gaze a moment longer than he was comfortable, then stared at the treetops. "Would you go back to Earth if they had done it?"

"Wow. Who wouldn't?" Alan picked a flower and absently fiddled with the petals. "I'd go in a heartbeat. I miss my cat."

"Sorry, I'm sure your cat misses you."

"Actually, I have several pets. I hope they are doing okay."

Scott remembered what the alien had told him when he was captured.

The memory often made him want to cry. He had not found anyone else who knew, but he hinted at the knowledge when meeting newcomers. "What if what if you knew that, if you went back to Earth, you'd die there?"

Alan's forehead wrinkled. "What? Why?"

"Never mind," said Scott, deciding to change the subject. If Alan had not been told, Scott was not going to spread bad news. "Anyway, I'm starving."

"Wow. Me too," agreed Alan.

"I saw the harvest team bring in a basket of Biting Nettle berries yesterday."

Alan smiled. "I heard those things taste like candy."

"They do! Want to go check if any are left?"

"Alright, let's go!" As if he was not as exhausted as Scott, Alan jumped to his feet and held out a hand to pull Scott up.

Scott clasped Alan's hand. A tingly shock made its way along his arm and through his body.

Before he could think too hard about it, he found himself yanked to his feet with little effort and strolling side by side with Alan to the fruit hut.

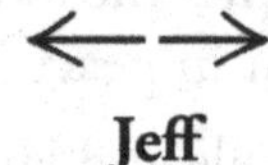

Jeff

Jeff dusted himself off, stretched, and headed back to camp as soon as the shuttle left. A little stiff from sitting so long while watching those fools perform his plan wrong. Now they were dead.

The only people he'd managed to convince to attack the aliens and gain access to the way home.

On Earth, he was careful to craft a perfect image of himself and his home life for the public. From the outside, he appeared as the real family man. A trophy wife - his third - and a teenage daughter. In reality, his daughter hated him, and he'd just found out his wife was cheating on him.

If he didn't return home, they would get all his money and live happy lives. He needed to get back before they declared him legally dead so he could divorce his wife, leaving her penniless, same as the last two.

These dead fools. They'd robbed him of his chance for revenge.

Setting aside plans for returning home, he instead focused on gaining power here in his current situation. He was still sleeping in a mud floor tent, and his clothing was reeking with sweat and spilled food.

Dave turned out helpful in finding him people to coerce. However, he was still maintaining the charade they were allies instead of treating Dave like an assistant. What he needed now was a proper subordinate, one he could order around to do his dirty work. It was important to remain aloof with complete deniability when caught.

With no money here, he could not hire someone. So, he would have to charm them. Or, a fan would work. He remembered the guy with curly hair. He would do.

Searching the camp, he finally found Alan near the fruit hut. The attractive boy was chatting with a tall young god of a boy, his honey-blond hair shining in the sunlight. Jeff recognized the boy with Alan as a friend of Olivia. He hoped his only known fan was not already part of the crowd of nature worshiping do-gooders.

He waited until they separated before approaching Alan, seemingly by accident. "Oh, look, it's my number one fan!"

Alan smiled a friendly greeting. "Ah, Mr. Phillips. How are you today?"

Jeff appreciated the respectful title, but he needed Alan to think they were buddies. "Alan, you can call me Jeff."

"Oh, wow! Thanks, Jeff."

"Come have a drink with me. I have something you'll want to hear. Believe me."

"Alright, great."

Dave and Jeff had moved their tents near each other and created a little space between them for meetings with various camp members. Jeff led Alan to this spot, pleased to find Dave already there, waiting with fresh juice.

"How did the ambush of the shuttle go?" Dave asked as he spread out a third mat and poured a third drink.

"Horrible. Twenty got cold feet, and the other six are dead."

"It would have gone better if they attacked together," said Alan.

"Totally disagree." Jeff shook his head. "With the guns on top and guards inside. I believe we need to move on from trying to get home."

Dave sighed. Jeff knew he wanted to get back to his ranch, and this would be a hard blow for the old man. He let his colleague have a moment to regain control of himself by turning to his newly acquired potential helper.

"What do you think about these extra hunting laws put in place by our so-called leaders?"

"I'm vegan, so personally, I don't need to hunt, but I don't care if others do. Probably should not hunt the big water lizards. They seem to dislike it."

"Do you agree the dictators who seized power should make those kinds of choices for everyone?"

"Wow, I had not thought about it before, but I suppose not. We should have elected officials if we're going to obey them without question."

"Yeah, we think alike."

"Exactly!" said Dave.

Jeff's eyebrows lowered, his forehead bunching a little in an expression he'd practiced in the mirror. He'd been told it was effective at making him appear both honest and worried.

"I should be one of the leaders, or maybe the only leader. I'm going to get elected, believe me."

"I have not heard anything about switching leaders. Is the camp holding elections?"

"No! That's the outrage. Those dishonest fakes are clinging to power and won't give it up."

"Wow, I had no idea. It doesn't seem right."

"We agree. So, we're working toward change. Will you join us?"

"Of course!"

Jeff grinned. It was too easy sometimes. "Our plan today is a protest," he said.

"Alright. Where? Like, at the meeting field?"

"Nope, in the river. We're going to take a bath."

Alan frowned for the first time. "No one is allowed to bathe in the river. It's the only source of salt-free water for the whole camp."

"That's a rule from those nature lovers. They just don't want people to think for themselves. Water flows down the river, so any water we use will be washed away."

"I guess it makes sense." Alan, still hesitant, had some of his eagerness back. "Let's do it! I could use a bath."

"The whole camp could." The grumbled comment by Dave caused both Jeff and Alan to laugh as they stood and started toward the river.

"So, Alan, tell us about yourself."

The fastest way to make an ally was to listen as they talked about themselves for as long as time allowed. Yet, Jeff almost immediately wished he had not asked.

Alan bragged about his clever door-opening cat, martial art skills, and job as a lead cashier. Next, he shared a long list of everything he'd ever found with his metal detector.

By the time they reached the river, Jeff was glad they were separating for privacy, but he was also pleased with the morning's work.

It only took six deaths to show him how the shuttle defenses operated. While he probably would not attempt another return home, it was good information to have. Also, he had two assistants now. Things were looking up.

CHAPTER 7

Olivia

Olivia was supposed to meet Scott and Finn at Dot's hut. She decided to make a quick detour to the river when the cut on her hand started bleeding again.

Kneeling to soak a rag in the water, she started thinking about her new friends. Scott's plan to meet and keep Finn awake together warmed her heart. She had never had such a caring friend, and this was another way Aeymay had provided her a kinder life than she'd been given on Earth.

Friendships never seemed to go right for her, but Scott didn't appear to notice her quirks, Dot didn't mind, and Finn kept hanging around.

Holding the rag to her hand, she took the path carved by all the humans to and from camp. In the last view of the sparkling water, through the trees, she caught sight of Jeff. Splashing in the river.

The beat of blood pounding in her injured hand sped up. How dare troublemakers break the rules so blatantly. She wanted to confront him, but where Jeff was, Dave and his knife could not be far away. She didn't need to add to the beating they already tried to give her that morning.

Turning away in disgust, she caught sight of their clothes. Jeff's suit and shirt. Dave's custom grass skirt and blue ball cap, and a third grass skirt. She didn't know who was with the two of them and didn't care. Anyone bathing in the river deserved a little karma in return.

She could not help grinning as she bent carefully, bruises from her fall screaming in protest, and gathered all the clothes to drape over an arm to carry back to camp. Even dangling Jeff's shoes from her good hand.

She knew where Jeff's tent was located. She'd seen the old man holding court there, with Dave to smooth the way.

Dave was generally level-headed and clever. Everyone liked Dave. Even Scott had a grudging respect for him. She wondered how many of the people coming to see Dave ended up under the spell of Jeff's charm.

Olivia shrugged, frustrated she was not as well-liked, according to Finn. She'd been so carefully cheerful, so friendly, and thought everything was going well, but recently people had been standoffish toward her. Worse, she'd been overwhelmed by her new community and attacked at a public meeting today. Perplexing.

She dumped the clothes in front of Jeff's tent. Hopefully, he'd take it as a warning not to repeat the action. Although, if he did, there was not much Olivia could do.

Weaving her way to Dot's tent, she saw groups buzzing with excited chatter. She would have thought they would still be sad the shuttle capture had failed, and while she saw a few unhappy faces, the bits and pieces of conversation overheard told a different story.

"I can sense water in the air."

"Everyone in my tent section says it's like having a sixth sense."

"I can't wait to get mine!"

Feeling separated from these people now, she could not cut in and ask.

Finding Dot, she sat cross-legged nearby, she adjusted the rag on her hand. It was warm now, but still helped stop blood from running everywhere.

"I have high hopes for this one," said Dot as she pushed mud around with nimble fingers in the shape of mug. "After it dries, I'm going to cover it with tree sap. Maybe it will hold water better."

"Nice. Hopefully, it stays in one piece."

"You went down hard this morning. Why aren't you resting."

"Didn't Scott tell you? We planned to meet here and tend to Finn. Also, I've been hearing odd chatter today that I don't understand. Do you know what's going on?"

"I do. Several people have come forward. They tell me they have been sensing things."

"What kind of things?"

"Some are sensing elements. Others are sensing people. Like, a friend they know headed toward them even before the person is in sight."

"It doesn't seem possible."

"It's happening to me too, actually. I've felt an incredible pull toward the forest. The only time I've followed this sensation, it has led me to an old building. A ruin from a past civilization."

Olivia laughed. "Guess a builder would be drawn to buildings. Still, I don't understand how this is happening."

"The people are saying these sixth senses are gifts from this new world."

"Does everyone have them?"

"As of today, I'd say yes, all the first waves of newcomers have them. Aren't you sensing anything extra?"

"Nope. I'm the same me."

Dot shrugged while waving Finn over. "Finn! Welcome. How are you doing?"

"I'm okay, I guess. Sleepy."

"Your body needs rest to heal, but let's keep you awake a little longer. Olivia and I were talking about the sixth sense. Apparently, she doesn't have one."

Finn carefully settled on the ground next to Olivia. "Really?"

"I've already spoken to Finn this morning. He can sense emotions. Especially strong ones," said Dot.

Olivia's anxiety rose with Finn sitting nearby. As conversation flowed on without her input, she missed the easy conversation she'd been having with Dot alone.

Why couldn't her brain make up its mind. Either it wanted friends or it didn't.

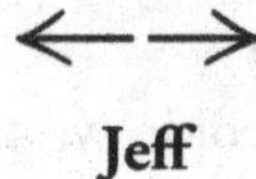

Jeff

"There you go, try this one." Dave handed over the finished work to Jeff.

Jeff hesitated before taking it. "It's not the same."

"Close enough," said Dave while tidying his workspace.

Jeff examined the leadership necklace. Some of the feathers were wrong, and the weave was not as tight, but at a glance? Dave was correct. It would be close enough.

"I think it looks great!" Alan reached out to stroke one of the longer feathers, and Jeff yanked the symbol of power out of reach.

Alan's constant enthusiasm grated on Jeff's nerves, and the boy was not even as useful as Jeff had hoped. "If you'd been able to steal one from the clothing hut, Dave would not have had to make me one."

Alan's head tilted, his nose crinkled, and he shrugged. "I did try."

Jeff noted he didn't even look upset at receiving the displeasure. This would not do. He needed the boy to fear him. If he could not threaten to fire him, he'd need something else. For now, though, he had bigger things to worry about. "When is the meeting?"

"The day after tomorrow, in the morning. No weapons allowed." Dave paused and glanced sideways at Jeff with some tightness to his lips. "Also, this time, we're gathering on the beach. Since the lizards will be around, we can't put any plans in motion to attack Olivia again because they might come to her aid. Agreed?"

Jeff frowned. He had been thinking of ways to work in a second beating at this coming meeting. Especially as he suspected her of stealing their clothes from the river. More critical was getting into a position of power. Dave had stopped his cleaning, staring at Jeff, apparently waiting for a reply. Jeff shrugged. "Who cares about the lazy girl. We've done enough damage to her reputation. Believe me, we don't need to worry about her anymore." It wasn't the truth, but Dave accepted it and returned to work.

Both Dave and Alan had turned out disappointing. With the announcement of new leader elections, he needed a lot of residents on his side. "How many people have agreed to my claim as a leader? What are the numbers?"

"None." Dave finally finished putting everything away, settled next to Alan for their planning session.

"None? What about the people we talked to yesterday? They seemed interested."

"When I talked to them later, they said you have potential, but no real plan for a community."

Jeff's grip on the new leadership necklace tightened, crushing some of the leaves. His subordinates in the past knew their jobs depended on how bad news was delivered. Dave should have sugar-coated it and mixed in praise. Instead, Jeff was forced to reply to a bald statement of negative facts.

It would be up to him to show he was the bigger man, as always.

He lifted his chin, puffed out his chest, and placed the necklace over his head. Arranging it carefully over his shoulders. "It's easy to look like a leader, and after you look the part, people will follow."

Alan raised a fist in the air and cheered.

Dave nodded. "Exactly."

"It doesn't matter if those phony leaders and the people have not seen me lead yet. When I go out today, and show what a good leader I am, the people will vote for me."

Jeff started immediately. Striding away from the meeting without another word, he followed the path toward the main areas of camp. This would work. It had worked in the past and would do so again. Acting like a leader equals getting hired as a leader.

Coming across some people chatting outside their tents, he approached them with shoulders back, displaying his new leadership symbol. "What are you doing sitting around with so much work to do. Clay huts won't build themselves."

The laughter of the group stopped. One started to speak, but Jeff cut him off. "You lot, go get the new digging shells and join the others in gathering the thick mud for new huts. Now."

They edged away from him, heading toward the tool hut.

Yes, this was good. Back in power, people doing his bidding without question. He'd had to dig mud yesterday with those stupid hand-sized fruit shells, and it was exhausting. As a leader, he'd never assign himself that task ever again.

With a new bounce to his step, he continued down the path.

When he came across the next group, he repeated his performance. Ordering them to, "Get out in the forest and harvest. Now."

They didn't argue, but they didn't look happy.

The path forked, with one direction toward the leadership tents and the other toward the river. He wondered if there would be anyone gathering water to order around and show off his leadership skills. At this rate, the whole camp would vote him in as leader.

Arriving at the edge of the river, he indeed saw a large group of people.

They were filling all the waterproof containers the castaways had been able to make. He'd been on this team before too. After gathering the water, they would place a container in each tent circle to easily access fresh water throughout the day. Getting into position and trying to think of an order for this group, he was spotted.

"Jeff? What are you doing with a leadership necklace?" The voice was not familiar. One of the old women Elders who didn't usually speak at the meetings.

He could not even remember the woman's name. "Of course, I have a leadership necklace. I'm the best leader here." He puffed out his chest again, showing off Dave's excellent work.

"We both know you are not a leader here. Take it off and hand it over. We don't want to confuse people when things are already tense."

The water collectors standing in the river stopped their careful work to watch the drama unfolding.

This was his chance. To show everyone what a good leader he could be. "What are you all staring at? Get back to work. Water won't jump into these containers by themselves." He was pleased with the resulting mix of stern and friendly tones.

One of the young boys scoffed at him. "You can't tell us what to do. Like she said, you're not a leader."

The old granny started moving at him again, reaching out, "Come on, give me the necklace. You know it's not for you."

There was no obvious way to stay in charge of this situation, and there was no way he was giving up so easily. He just needed to find the right spin on this, the right words to say. He just needed time. Jeff backed up, forgetting how close he was to the river and fell backward with a huge splash.

In this deeper part of the river, he sank like a stone. As the current moved him into the range of the shallower section and the water team, several hands grabbed him and pulled.

Gasping for air and about to give his thanks for a timely rescue, he faltered. Everyone was laughing. All of them. Some doubled over.

He didn't understand their laughter. It could be a bit funny to watch someone fall into a river, but it didn't deserve this much enjoyment.

The boy standing next to him, stripped down to underwear for this task, pointed downstream and said, "The river stole your hair, buddy."

Jeff gasped. The loss of air in the river nothing to the fear stealing the breath from his lungs. He watched as a small mat of hair floated smoothly away from the gathered people. No. It could not be his.

When he felt around at his bald head, the water team began laughing all over again.

Desperate to get away, to regroup, he pulled himself from the grasp of boys holding him upright and scrambled onto the bank.

At the top, he could not think of anything to say, and they were still laughing anyway. He straightened his shoulders and left.

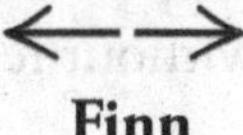

Finn

"Finn!" Scott called several times, and Finn halted before going to the food hut.

What could be happening now, Finn wondered. "Is everything okay?"

"I got this for you." Scott bent over to catch his breath, but held out the translation guide. Scott was fit. If he'd become out of breath, he must have been in a hurry.

"Thanks?" Finn accepted the book with furrowed eyebrows. Staring down at the two symbols on the front, he could now read as "Blue Kin."

"My extra sense developed. I know what others need even if they don't ask. It's been happening all day. I had an urgent feeling you'd need the book."

"I appreciate the effort, but I don't think I'll need it. I'm not even planning to go on my usual beach run today."

"Well, you have it now. Always better to prepare ahead. Oh, and return it to Olivia when you are done. I had to borrow it from her tent."

"Okay, will do."

Scott's eyes glazed, and he jogged off with a wave. "Gotta go, see ya later!"

Finn shook his head. People all over the camp were acting oddly today as their gifts settled in. His gift had apparently arrived a couple days early, so he was already learning to control it. He could choose when to sense emotions or back away and block himself off from them. Poor Scott would get there too, and in the meantime, lots of people would be assisted today.

Returning to his task of fruit prep, he limped through the doorway of one of the only fully walled huts. Letting his eyes adjust to the shadowy interior, he gasped at the sight of a single Blue Kin lizard munching on fruit.

The creature had pulled one of the larger tree fruits from a basket and used his claws to pry it open and lick out the juice inside. Now he could see better, this lizard was small compared to the others. A youth, probably. Old enough for forest foraging alone, but just barely.

Finn carefully crept to the opposite side of the tent and sat. The Blue Kin watched him, apparently without fear, and then returned attention to the fruit.

Feeling a weight in his hand, he remembered the translation guide and Scott's insistence he'd need it. Flipping through the guide awkwardly with his splinted fingers, he found the page with the symbol for hello and began drawing it in the dirt with his good hand.

In his peripheral vision, he saw the lizard's orange antenna point up and forward with interest. Eyes bright and curious. It skittered over to him, coming around to read the symbol.

The Blue Kin quivered, its antenna twitching, and copied the symbol. Glancing at him for approval as it scratched at the ground, several claws getting in the way of its longest claw.

Finn wondered if this youth could only copy or if it knew the language. He marked the symbol for name, but there was nothing in the guide for letters, only concepts. He chose a name for himself on the spot and added the symbol for clouds.

The little creature next to him hopped from foot to foot. He copied the symbol for a name next to a new symbol.

Finn flipped through the pages until he found something close. It meant Flat Water.

The lizard was apparently able to read some of his confusion. He retrieved the fruit, finished breaking it open, and let the juice pool next to the symbol in a puddle.

Puddles! Finn was sure he had it. He opened his senses up and could feel the rightness of it. As well as the friendliness and cheer coming from the little youth.

For the first time, in realizing their emotions were so similar to a human, he began to think of the Blue Kin as people. It shamed him that simply knowing they were intelligent was not enough, but he understood now.

Wondering what else to chat about with an intelligent alien, he flipped through the book for inspiration. He came across a symbol for love, so he wiped away their last words and wrote, "Myself Love Fruit."

Puddles repeated the symbol for myself, and with a wiggle, began licking the fruit again while keeping eye contact, then swiped out the last word and wrote two more.

Finn translated them as Difficult and Capture. He puzzled over this until Puddles pushed the fruit toward him. It was the same one he and Olivia had gone through so much trouble to gather. When these fruits were knocked from a tree, they splattered to the ground below.

They were indeed difficult to capture, but what an odd way to phrase it. He wondered who created this imprecise translation guide, hoping eventually, if he got good enough, he could perhaps create a better one.

He drew the symbol for agreement.

Puddle's attention switched as if hearing something far away. He drew the symbol for goodbye, skittered over to grab another tree fruit in its jaw, and, holding the treasure high, ran from the hut.

Finn sagged back against the hut wall. The unexpected encounter cheered him. He vowed to learn this native language without needing the guidebook. Finn wanted to talk to all the lizards and become friends with more of them.

Also, the Blue Kin might have knowledge about how the forest worked here and what plants were deadly. If they could communicate better with the Blue Kin and perhaps build some kind of peace with them, only good could come of it.

He would have to track Scott down and tell him how important his assistance was today. Both for his future with the Blue Kin and the future of all humans here on this planet.

CHAPTER 8

Jeff

Jeff knew he was sulking. With his suit damaged beyond repair, his spray tan gone, and his toupee lost to the river, he didn't feel very dominant anymore. Now he looked like an old man.

With his confidence failing, all his plans for pursuing leadership at the meeting crumbled around him. Over the last two days of hiding in his tent, Alan had been tending his needs, bringing food and water.

He could not show his face, or more precisely his bald head, to the people he would one day rule over. Appearances must be maintained.

As the light began to fill his tent, he wondered if the few people at the river who saw him in disgrace could be quietly murdered. Although, at the moment though he didn't have anyone he trusted enough to perform this basic task, or money to pay them.

That would change. It must change. He built himself up from nothing once. He could do it again.

Today was the new leadership meeting. Jeff scolded himself for wasting time in self-pity. Now he only had hours left to organize his return to power.

First, he needed to get out of bed. Then coordinate with Dave and Alan to find a path forward from this mess.

He burst into Dave's tent, hoping to shock the man into waking, but Dave was already busy even though it was early morning. Well before Jeff would usually stir from sleep.

Alan was with him, and their nimble fingers were working on opposite ends of the same project. Extra vines and leaves scattered around them.

"What are you doing playing with leaves? The meeting is today, and we need to make some action plans."

Dave pulled from his intense focus, yawned, and rubbed his eyes, but his voice was clear and soothing. "I've made you a crown of leaves for your clever head."

Alan glanced quickly at Dave, and Jeff thought he saw his eyes narrow at the comment, but Alan smiled at Jeff, saying, "I'm glad you are feeling better. It's good you up and about. We've been working on this for you all morning. Nearly finished."

Jeff's eyes went wide. Initiative? From these two? Perhaps he'd picked his crew better than he'd thought. He was almost touched, but remembered he was the best at hiring, so this was a win for his own skills at choosing talented employees.

He sat on Dave's sleeping mat, watching them finish the crown. A crown! Perfect.

He daydreamed of arriving at the meeting in the beautiful orange crown and all the castaways realizing how important he was to their future. Everyone voted for him as the only leader. Not the leader of any individual village or camp, but the ruler of them all.

Like when he was in charge of all the banks. He was not head of one bank. He was the head of many banks. It would be the same here, he decided.

The best way to become a leader was to take Dot's place as head of the main camp. From there, he could influence the eventual break away camps leaving to create towns.

With access to the ocean and river, and influence over the arriving newcomers, this main camp was obviously the seat of power. As a leader here, he would bargain with the other villages and eventually rule over them. As he took over each one, he could put his people in place to run the villages as he wanted them to run. He would rule as king.

He would be back to living in luxury soon. "With my big brain, we can make the best plan," he announced.

"The quickest way to get people to come together is to unite them against something else. Since turning the camp against Olivia didn't have the outcome we hoped, perhaps we could make the aliens a threat, so others would join you against them, sir?" Dave suggested.

Jeff raised his eyebrows at Dave's use of sir, but was glad Dave finally showed him the respect he required.

"Yeah, sounds good. We can make the greatest plan ever. We'll come out of this meeting in charge of Main Camp."

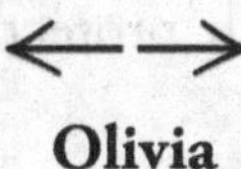

Olivia

Unable to sleep, Olivia had been watching the camp come slowly to life from under a tree on a slight rise.

She could see most of the meadow from here, the tent tops covering what was a beautiful wonderland when less than a hundred people filled it. Now turned into barren wasteland when used to contain double that amount.

Unfocusing, she let her fingers weave the basket in her lap without her full attention. The healing cut on her hand slowed her down, but didn't keep her from the task.

She watched the noisy people going to the river with waterproofed baskets, some heading to the ocean probably for a quick morning bath, others starting smoky cookfires. Smiling at the sight of a Blue Kin trotting out of the food tent with a tree fruit held in its mouth.

She felt comfortable around the lizards. Lounging with them on the beach. Life was so peaceful when she could pretend she was one of the Blue Kin.

Humans, she didn't understand at all. Not the people who died needlessly trying to attack the shuttle, or the people who missed money, or the people who didn't see how amazing Aeymay could be and the opportunities it represented.

Worse, humans over-complicated the simplest of things. Insisting on concepts like ownership and money. The Blue Kin lived with the land. They didn't need fancy houses or high-paying jobs. They ate food the land provided. Humans could do the same. The Blue Kin lived among the trees. Humans could do that too. They bathed in the ocean and played with their children. Olivia longed for life so simple.

In that longing, she realized something important.

Everyone has their own longings. Maybe she was dreaming of simplicity, but others might be dreaming of a big fancy house. The views she shared with Dot, perhaps they were not for everyone.

Everything had always been so clear in Olivia's worldview. Good and evil. Right and wrong.

The environment was worth protecting. Both on Earth and here on Aeymay.

The old and rich should not be in charge.

Religion was tearing apart the world at the seams.

She was right, and they were wrong.

However, she respected her mother's choice to practice her religion and her dad's freedom to own a gun. Dot was both old and not evil. Actually, Olivia overworked the environment too, with her books made from trees and her electronics the product of terrible mining practices. Hypocrite.

Everything was hopelessly muddled. Nothing was black and white. It wasn't even grey. Bright splashes of color, blending in ways she didn't want to look at.

This must be what Dot was trying to tell her yesterday. She didn't understand why Dot would release the small amount of power she held, keeping all these humans in check, and instead let them choose leaders who would ruin everything. Except, what she saw as destroying, those people saw as progress toward their dreams.

She'd been unhappy growing up in the worldview of the rich old guys running the country. Others would be just as unhappy forced into her views.

People like Jeff could never be happy with the serenity the Blue Kin enjoyed in their simple life.

Aeymay was big. It might be possible for everyone to live how they wanted without getting in the way of each other. Maybe she could live a simple life, and others could go off and live their complicated lives.

Dot understood it would be better to have people of the same mind living together, instead of making everyone follow one set of rules. It hurt, to accept this new reality, and Olivia mourned her vision of a perfect human civilization.

More humans were emerging from their tents to start the day. Buzzing all over the meadow like flies on a carcass.

The second chance she'd seen for humans was falling apart as they repeated history. Although, all of these annoying people were planning to leave Main Camp. What a relief to have them gone.

Finn flashed through her mind. Would he leave too? Seeing his little hula dance when they first met, his smile as he caught the fruits she dropped toward him, remembering their firelit party and the feel of his hands on her hips, her arms around his neck. Protecting each other from the crowd. Olivia admitted she would miss Finn, when he left with the others.

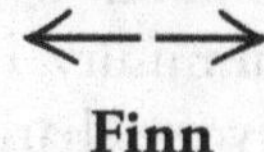

Finn

On the way to return the translation guide, Finn saw Olivia sitting alone under a tree rather than resting in her tent.

As he got closer. He tentatively reached out his new sense, but pulled back from Olivia's swirl of frustration and sadness.

"Hey, you. Plotting the takeover of all you see before you?" Finn asked, carefully sitting down next to her. His ribs ached, and he tried not to groan out loud.

"Yes, actually. Well, kind of. I don't plan to flee with the others. I've made friends among the Blue Kin. So, if all the annoying people could just leave, I could be happy, even if I'm in a camp of one."

Loneliness and hurt rolled off Olivia, so strongly Finn could not block it all. "I was just, returning this book. Scott asked me to give it to you."

"Thanks." Olivia accepted the book. Settling it under her basket, she returned to weaving.

Finn waited, but no comments followed. Nothing blunt or cheerful to say. In fact, Finn noticed for the first time since he'd had this new skill that Olivia's words matched her emotions. He didn't know what had changed this morning, but maybe now was a good time for a real conversation. "Do you hate me?"

"What? Why would I?" Olivia didn't look up from weaving, but her highbrows had shot into her forehead.

"What you said, when we met, and later."

"Ignore me. Besides, I never said I hate you."

"So, what's wrong?"

"I'm coming to realize people have different goals than mine, and maybe that's okay. I understand now. Dot can't get everyone to comply with our dream. I don't even want that anymore. Instead, I'm hoping everyone goes away to create whatever vision they want for themselves, and I can stay here and talk to new arrivals. Maybe some of them will want to start a little community with me."

"What would that be like?" asked Finn.

"Kind of what I said before about living in tribes, but that vision was for everyone. Instead, the community I want to build would have one small like-minded village. Everyone sharing resources and meals, equal in their duties and free time. No one in charge."

"It sounds peaceful."

Olivia sighed. "It would be peaceful. If people with the same ideals came together for it. If I could find people willing to create it with me."

"I think I could live like that." Fiddling with the grass on his skirt, he could sense the hope rise in Olivia, and when she looked up, their eyes met and held.

"Hello!" Scott ran over to them, as out of breath as he'd been when Finn saw him that morning. Scott dropped onto his back, stretching out with an arm flopped over his eyes. "I sensed you needed me. What's wrong? Are you okay?"

Finn laughed. "I don't know if we need you. Although the book you brought me came in handy. I had a conversation with a Blue Kin youth named Puddles in the food hut."

"Well, good." Scott stretched his arms and yawned, sitting upright to complete the circle of three. "I'm doing great at knowing what people need today, and it's good we're talking to the Blue Kin more."

Olivia started basket weaving again, thinking out loud. "I'm worried for them. If one of the communities unfriendly to the Blue Kin stays in Main Camp or too near them. I think another clash would end badly for the Kin and the humans."

"Well, the lizards have a right to defend themselves, but I'm worried too," said Scott.

Half of an idea started to form for Finn, if he could connect all the dots. "Maybe people friendly to the Kin should take over Main Camp. To protect them?"

Scott shook his head and yawned again. "As far as I know, people who still like the Kin are a small group. I mean, count me in, but it would be a tiny village."

Finn's idea finished forming, and he said, "Or, a little community. Olivia, you should do it. You should take over the leadership of Main Camp to set up your community. You'd have all the Blue Kin defenders to start and access to newcomers, so they could hear your idea and stay with us or move on to other villages."

"Us?" Olivia asked, and Finn felt her hope surge again.

Finn smiled at her. "Yes, the three of us, the core of the community."

Scott rubbed his hands together and leaped up. "Sounds good to me. I'll go talk to a few buddies about it, so you'll have some votes at the meeting. See you there!"

When Scott was out of hearing range Finn said, "It sounds good to me too. I think we work well together."

Olivia's hands stilled again. She didn't look up again, but Finn knew some of her loneliness had been replaced with delight.

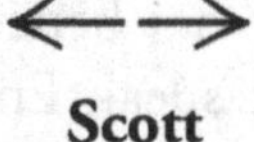

Scott

Scott felt the pull of another task. It was rather like being drawn toward a fireplace after coming in from the cold. A physical need and he could not stop himself from leaning into the urge to help.

Mostly he'd been delivering objects. What was even stranger was delivering himself. First to Finn, and now toward the bay. When he arrived, he didn't see anyone, but the pull dragged him along the tree line until he noticed Alan.

The boy had been captivating his imagination since the first time they had spoken. Remembering Alan's natural curls and beautiful brown eyes under thick lashes. He'd only spoken with Alan twice, but was now sensitive to the other boy's wanderings and often saw him around and outside of camp.

As Scott got closer, their eyes met. A joy filled Scott's chest as he sucked in air and he could not help but smile. His eyes crinkling. His head lightweight, as if filled with helium. All he wanted to do was run fingers through the soft curls and whisper in Alan's ear all the things perfect about him.

"Hi Scott, I was just going to go find you."

Scott pushed away the distracting thoughts. "Well, here I am. No looking required."

Scott wanted to sit far from temptation, but found himself almost touching knees with Alan after getting settled. Had he misjudged the distance, or had Alan moved closer?

"I'm worried and need to tell you something."

"Why me?" As honored as Scott was with this apparent trust, he barely knew Alan and could not think what information the boy might share.

"I'm worried," Alan repeated. "About the Blue Kin. It's said they are attending the meeting today, and Jeff intends to rile the crowd against them."

Scott held in a frown. This was a new side of Alan. So far, he'd seen the self-assured boy act friendly and jaunty all over camp. Worried, though?

He realized he was wool-gathering again and replied, "I haven't heard the Blue Kin are attending. What benefit could they get from attending a human meeting? They don't speak English, and I'm the only one who could translate for them. If they even cared."

"It's something Dave told Jeff. Actually, Dave has been acting odd the last couple of days."

"Everyone has been acting odd, with all the extra senses developing."

Alan smiled shyly. "Do you have an extra sense?"

"It's what brought me to you this morning."

Alan leaned forward. Eyebrows raised slightly. "How?"

"I sense when people need things. I guess I sensed you needed me."

"Perhaps I do, and not just this morning."

Scott's jaw dropped while he searched for something to say. Was Alan flirting with him?

Alan didn't back down, keeping the ground he'd gained when getting too close. "The main reason I was planning to look for you is that I need you to warn your friend, Dot. Jeff wants to take over Main Camp and has some pretty awful plans to do it. Most of those happen at the meeting soon."

"Well, he can't have Main Camp. I've already signed on as a member of the group staying at Main Camp under Olivia's leadership."

Alan groaned. "I'm happy for you, and Olivia, and even for the Blue Kin, but Jeff will flip at this news."

Scott swallowed hard, but dove in. "You don't have to stay with Jeff's gang. You could, um, join me. I mean, join Olivia, staying in Main Camp."

Alan smiled slowly, his thick curved eyelashes downcast for a moment, on full display. Instead of replying, he brushed Scott's hand with his own as he stood to leave.

"You know, all of Jeff's plans would be thwarted if Olivia claimed Main Camp first. Pass on the word to Dot, let Olivia speak first, and I think we'll have a smooth meeting."

"Will do." Scott leaned back on an elbow to watch the other boy leave. Alan's glowing olive skin on his broad bare back beaded with sweat. His curls bouncing and narrow hips swaying attractively in the full grass skirt.

CHAPTER 9

Olivia

"Settle down, everyone, settle down. This will be a long meeting, but it will be our last together." The meetings were always well attended, but today Dot spoke to every human on the planet.

"As you know, we've grown too big for the small camp that started this new human civilization. We're going to break apart into various types of settlements. Anyone with an idea is welcome to speak. If the person's idea and suggestion of land to stake have the support of five other people, they can stand in a group. Others can join them at any time through the meeting. By the end of the meeting, everyone must pick a group. Raise your hand if you understand this process."

Everyone raised their hand, so Dot continued. "After a group is formed, in front of everyone by show of hands, the new group will elect the leader as the first mayor of their new village. The mayor will be in charge of creating and enforcing rules and can be replaced at any time if more than half the community votes to replace them. Does anyone have questions? No? Okay, our first speaker is Olivia."

Dot ignored the quiet booing coming from several attendees and waved Olivia forward. Olivia looked over the crowd as she walked to the front, seeing some familiar faces and a few new faces. Not many friendly faces.

Jeff sat tall, glaring at her. Around his head was a mass of orange leaves, some woven together, sticking up like multiple ears. Amazed at this shocking bit of headgear, she let her gaze drift again and saw Finn smiling reassuringly.

Standing near Dot, with two hundred sets of eyes on her, she froze.

At more than double the amount of people she had to speak to at the last meeting, she could not seem to catch a full breath to start speaking. With her heart beating too fast, the crowd started going in and out of focus. The moment to talk came and went. She remembered the goals, a family of friends, keeping Finn here, and protecting the Blue Kin. Mentally tossing her practiced speech away, she spoke with simple passion from the heart.

"In a community, we will live lightly on the land with houses crafted from what we can gather. Like grass, mud, and sand. All chores will rotate, so everyone has plenty of free time. Communal meals made from fruits and greens. Our only law will be Harm None."

The silence after she finished speaking stretched out in her mind, and for a panicked moment, she thought no one would stand with her. Then Scott joined her with two other boys, and Finn, next a few elders with Dot among them. It was more than the required five.

As the meeting host Dot stepped away from Olivia, moving back to her spot at the head of the meeting, asking, "Do you have a land claim in mind?"

"We want to claim Main Camp. Our community would continue being responsible for greeting newcomers and also establishing peace with the lizard-like Blue Kin."

Dot turned to the crowd, "Does everyone agree to this land claim?"

"I don't want to live by those scary creatures!" shouted someone in the crowd.

"Better them than us!" someone else agreed.

Dot nodded at the comments. "Olivia, you have gained your land claim and may form a group. Does everyone in your group elect you as mayor?" All voted yes with a raised hand.

Leaving Dot to finish the meeting, her last role as a leader, Olivia led the rest of her new family some steps away and drew a line in the sand for others to join them. No one did.

The second person stood to appeal to the crowd, but Olivia didn't hear them. She had a headache. Being required to talk in front of so many people, her blood was still pounding with anxiety. She had some excitement too. Her little village was going to happen. Five was enough to get started, and she was sure other newcomers would join eventually.

She tried to ignore the weight of being in charge of other lives and knowing she'd now have to deliver on the ideals she'd been spouting this whole time. With Dot's help, she was sure she could do it. Of course, Scott was proving a valuable friend too, and Finn?

She glanced sideways at him, but he was intently watching the ongoing spectacle. She supposed she should be paying attention too. The man speaking was one of those constantly hounding Dot about allowing money and trading. Olivia remembered this was the group Finn had planned to join and hoped he didn't regret his choice.

The man outlined a modern small town. With a sturdy economy, good-paying jobs, neighborhood housing with big backyards, a downtown strip of shops, and more. The land stake would be a valley found a one-day walk from the beach, with a section of the river running close enough to be useful, but not close enough to flood. After his land claim was granted, half the population stood and joined him behind his line.

The next group took half the remaining people with it. An older boy voted in as leader described a trading community, with a land stake further up the beach. So, they could still live near the productive coastline, but away from the natives.

Dot stood in front of the remaining undecided people. "The rest of you must pick a group now or stay in Main Camp until you know which community you want to join."

Scott leaned toward Olivia and said, "Feels like the end of an era. The beginning of humans spreading over an unprepared planet of natives."

Olivia agreed. "It does feel like we're releasing danger out into the world, but I have to remember we cannot control the actions of everyone, only ourselves."

Speaking of stupid actions, she thought of Jeff and his crew. She didn't see which group they'd ended up in, but she didn't care. Only glad she would never have to deal with Jeff ever again.

She flipped around to greet her new group, and her stomach sank. In the shuffle of newcomers, she'd gained around twenty people - most of them from the undecided group - but three of those people were Alan, Dave, and Jeff.

Jeff's pouting turned to smugly curled lips when he saw Olivia's shock at finding him there.

Why would the most vocal against Olivia's ideals choose her group?

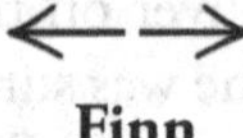

Finn

Finn crossed his arms. "You already know I'm no chef."

"Right, but you wanted jam. So, you can make it." Olivia wiggled her eyebrows at him in a mock challenge.

Finn laughed. "I can try, but why? With so many important tasks to do, what possible use could jam have?"

"I want to have a party tonight."

"A what?" Finn's eyes went round.

"Party: a festival, a social gathering of people."

"Funny. I mean, why."

Olivia smiled and clapped her hands, her determination plus unease obvious to Finn's new senses. "Team spirit!" she said. "If we can cook anything a little different, out of the ordinary, it will feel more like we have something to celebrate on our first night alone together."

"The camp is so empty, with everyone gone. Even the ten newcomers all went with them." Finn held in a shudder at how alone they were, here in the dark night of an alien planet with only a handful of humans remaining at Main Camp. Olivia's uncertainty didn't help.

"There will be others," she said. "Our community will grow." Olivia twisted the hard fruit shells in her hand. "Here, I brought you these. I thought maybe you could use them in your jam-making. You can't put them directly in the fire, but maybe near enough to cook the berries?"

"It could work. Any favorite flavor?" he asked, examining the hard half-circle shells she'd brought him.

"None of those icky scary plant berries. They still creep me out."

"The Biting Nettle fruits? Have you at least tried them?"

Olivia squinted her eyes and stuck out her tongue. "No way, with their little curly hairs and bumpy forms? I'll pass."

"You can't even tell the hairs are there while you eat them. You are missing out. It's some of the tastiest fruit on Aeymay."

"More for you." Olivia wrinkled her nose one more time, but drifted off in thought. When her resolve hardened, she spoke again. "Can I ask you something?"

"Sure." Finn busied himself getting the fire built higher, giving Olivia a moment to collect herself.

"Why did you stay? Here is my group. Was it only that you liked my community idea?"

Finn considered what to say and settled on the straight facts, or most of them. "It's true, your community idea sometimes still terrifies me, and if I'm not cut out to live in a tribe, I'll go join the town. However, I would like to try, and more, I want to live near the Blue Kin."

The answer surprised Olivia, so he continued. "I never told you what my life plan was. I wanted to become a veterinarian. I'm interested in animals. Finding a talking animal and wrapping my mind around the idea it's not an animal. I don't know. It's changed things for me. I want to study them. I want to learn the language. I want to be their friend."

There was a third reason he didn't plan to say aloud. He was glad Olivia could not sense his thoughts, or she'd find out how charmed he was by the messy spikes of her short red hair or how lost he could become in her hazel eyes.

He would find a way to not only survive in this community, but perhaps live happily here. While also studying an entire native sentient population.

Olivia considered his words, then smiled and ruffled her pixie cut into even more of a mess. "Okay, Mr. Gloomy, I'll take that as an answer. For now."

"I'm not gloomy, but you're still annoyingly hopeful."

"Don't call me that," Olivia said.

"Or what?"

"I'll pour jam down your shirt while you sleep."

"I don't wear a shirt anymore, but you are welcome to have a go at my boxer shorts."

"Not in a million years." Olivia flung a thin piece of driftwood at him from the stack by the fire.

Finn dodged, shouting, "Hey! I've been attacked!"

"Get out of my kitchen," Olivia announced.

"I would if it had any walls," replied Finn. "Besides, I'm making jam."

After their open conversation, yesterday before the meeting and just now, he thought they'd turned a corner in their relationship. Finn was both irritated and amused at her antics and their almost argument. He sighed and started smashing berries into one of the bowls. Living near Olivia would be entertaining.

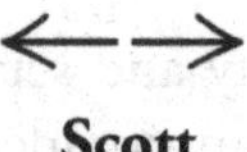

Scott

Scott sat outside his tent, a small distance from the cook fire, and watched Finn speak quietly with Olivia.

After a long day of hard work, the warm night air made him drowsy. Scott felt happy. Everything was right with the world now.

The massive crowd of people gone and the Blue Kin were understanding the symbols he drew. Finn and Olivia finally seemed on a path to getting along. Best of all, Alan had stayed in Main Camp.

Alan plopped down close to him. Startling Scott into bracing a hand on Alan's knee. He started to pull the hand away, but Alan covered it and held it in place.

Not sure what to say, Scott was saved by a loud argument. Olivia's raised voice saying, "Get out of my kitchen."

"Ooh, love in the air," said Alan. The tone was mocking, but the gaze he held made Scott's breath stop.

"I want to show you something," said Scott. This time pulling Alan to his feet and into the forest.

As they left the fires behind, their eyes adjusted to the dark. Starlight led the way, shining from between the treetops.

"I'm not sure if you heard, but Dot's sixth sense is being able to detect buildings. I don't think the quick grass huts count, so she's been drawn to exploring the forest."

"Buildings? In this forest?"

"Some past civilization built and abandoned them."

"I've explored the forest a lot. Why haven't I found any?"

"They build them mostly underground, and the doors are not obvious.

Dot showed me one, quite close to camp. It's a small one, and no one knows about it except Dot."

"Sounds private."

"Extremely." Scott gathered some vines out of the way and let Alan pass. On the other side of the tree covered in vines was a small cave opening.

Ducking almost bent in half to enter, the floor sloped downward until it opened into a space they could stand in. Roughly the size of Scott's bedroom on Earth.

The shadowy white woven walls were made of some kind of stringy paper webbing, with symbols and pictures drawn onto them, the bare ground uneven, but polished smooth. Glowing mushrooms planted along the edges of the ceiling gave the room an enchanting dreamy glow.

Scott fell back on facts while he worked up the courage to do what he came here for. "A few of the ruins are quite large, with long tunnels."

"Do you think the caves were already here, or the other people dug them out?" Alan stayed close, but explored the room by craning his neck to stare all around and then at the ceiling mushrooms.

"Well, no one knows if the caves are natural or created. Or, why they are different sizes. This one is small. Just this room."

"Cozy."

"Very."

Scott shifted closer to Alan, drawn by his intoxicating scent, moving slow and savoring the details highlighted in the bioluminescence around them. The dimple in Alan's cheek, the parting of his lips as his breathing sped up, the contrast of his white teeth in the shadowy space.

Finally getting close enough to stare directly into Alan's eyes, Scott breathed in the heady sweetness of Alan until he felt dizzy.

He might have stayed frozen there forever, but Alan leaned forward and kissed Scott's cheek. Then pulled back, darting his eyes up to discover how this affection was received.

Scott gently gripped the boy's jaw with both his hands and pulled him into a deep kiss. In answer, Alan pushed Scott against the wall, wrapping arms around his neck, and kissed him back.

When they were both out of air, Scott said, "Hey, Metal Detector Guy,

I think we should get back to camp." Still chest to chest, he felt Alan shake with laughter.

"Alright, I guess so. I heard something about a party." Alan lifted his head, kissing Scott's cheek again.

Scott ran his hand through Alan's curls. "We could come back here, sometime."

Alan's face lit with the smile that had enchanted Scott when they first met, and he said, "I'd like that."

CHAPTER 10

Jeff

Jeff was upset. Miserable even. Pacing in his tent helped. Ordering Dave around also relieved some of the stress.

The meeting had not gone how he wanted. Jeff's plans hinged on getting called to speak before anyone else claimed Main Camp, but he didn't realize it until Olivia asked for Main Camp.

Everything moved so fast, and in the end, he'd had to join this disgusting commune. The only way to keep moving forward was to ensure everyone was as miserable as himself.

His first act as its new member was to have Dave kill one of the docile toothless alligator things from upriver and tan it to make him a sleeveless shirt.

"The shirt is stiff and scratchy," he told Dave.

"Sorry, sir. Would you like your old shirt?"

"No, no. It's tattered trash and not worthy of me. Besides, Olivia's face every time she sees me in the new shirt is priceless. No. This shirt is stiff, but I'll wear it until Olivia stops looking irritated about it."

With his suit finally unusable and the days heating up, he needed a wardrobe to revamp. This uncomfortable shirt was just the start.

"How are the shorts coming along? I refuse to continue wearing skirts like a woman."

"Nearly finished, sir."

His shoes, no longer shiny, were still functional enough to wear, even if he seemed out of place as the only person not barefoot here. His tall calf-high socks were holding up as well. Even if they were overheating, they did have the added benefit of protecting his lower legs from sunburn.

He examined his broken watch. The glass had cracked on a rock some days earlier, but it was still working and did have diamonds inset into it. He decided he'd miss the weight of it, so he left it on.

His new crowns made by Dave were perfect for covering the fact he'd lost his hair, and they were protecting him from sunburn as well. Parts of him, at least, the rest of him was not so lucky. Especially his nose, arms, and knees.

He tried to stay out of the sun, but Olivia kept assigning him chores in the middle of the afternoon. He could use the cleaned mud the others used, but refused to cover himself in mud like a swamp person.

Dave came over with his new pants. "There you go. It's a modified version of the grass skirt, and I think your old belt - the one you insisted I include - adds a unique flair."

Getting the shorts on to complete his ensemble was the mood boost he needed. He wished he had a mirror. All he was missing for a complete look was a leadership necklace, but now he was dressed for the part, so it would happen soon.

"Now, I look like a leader. I'm so handsome. Where is Alan? He's missing the big reveal."

Dave shrugged. "I believe he's spending most of his free time out in the forest."

"Probably with that silly metal detector. As if it could pick up alien metals."

"Actually, and I could be wrong, but I think all the elements on Earth are the same ones found anywhere in the universe."

"Sounds ridiculous. You must be wrong."

Dave nodded and shrugged politely with his head lowered respectfully.

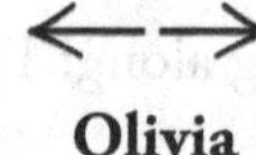

Olivia

Olivia stomped and stomped and stomped some more. The wet mud under her feet squished between her toes. She backed away to let Dot add more water and started stomping again with renewed vigor.

The tall trees surrounding her shaded their work and would do the same over the years for the community center they were building. As the first human building in Aeymay, this task was a perfect blend of Olivia's sketching skills for the construction plans and Dot's lifetime of knowledge in alternative building materials.

She'd seen Dot shape mud in her hands to make cups and bowls, but now the elder was going to show her how to shape a whole house. They blended the clay with sand, dried grass, and water by foot-power alone since tools were scarce.

Every enraged stomp she pounded into the mud gave her a hit of stress relief. This might be her new favorite hobby. She pictured all her problems in the mud and flattened them beneath her heel.

Finn being unfriendly again after the jam incident? Squish.

The people in her new village not listening to a word she said? Smash.

Jeff causing more trouble than even Olivia could have anticipated? Splat.

"Good grief, Olivia," said Dot. "Perhaps a little less jumping and splashing? You look like an angry toddler in a rain puddle."

Olivia froze and blushed, gazing down and blinking away tears, and watched her mentor doing the same process she should be doing. Dot massaged the mud rhythmically, like a cat kneading a blanket. Blending the muddy mixture with her toes and heels as deftly as she'd seen the woman do with her fingers and palms. Dot's pile of mud looked like ready building material. Olivia's was a sloppy mess.

"Don't worry about it. You just need more practice," said Dot.

"Fine. I didn't know your sixth sense was mind reading." Olivia tried not to pout. It was already a bad day in a bad week, but she didn't want Dot to see her sulking.

"I don't need to read minds to know you think your pile looks like crap. Every person starting out feels the same. Give it time and keep practicing. I was once in your shoes, learning from a master at cob building. I thought I'd never get it. We're just lucky this planet has clay mud, so give it time, and one day you'll be teaching a generation of youngsters."

Olivia smiled and returned to squishing the mud. Refraining from stomping so hard, but she still could not match Dot's grace. "Do you think we'll get the base finished today?"

"No. These houses take time and effort."

"Not like the grass and vine houses going up all over the meadow, right?" Olivia could hear the whiny note in her voice, but could not remove it. "I announced at the party that I have specific places I wanted buildings and houses to go, and everyone agreed, but now they are building all over the place. Not even the sturdy building structures you approved of. Hasty and random!"

"All you can control is you."

Dot's often used phrase, so wise and profound at times, grated on Olivia's temper today. Yes, she could only control herself, but these people had made her mayor and agreed to follow her rules. Of course, she had said the only rule would be Harm None, and yet, other laws were implied by the type of community she'd outlined.

"In village building news, Jeff is asking for approval and assistance in building a large woven grass hut to share with Dave."

"Don't get me started on Jeff and Dave. They are blatantly breaking the rules."

"Interesting. What rules are those." Dot's bland tone didn't fool Olivia. She could tell the old lady was trying to make a point.

"Harm None. The rule is Harm None, and they killed a river creature." Olivia pressed lips together and rubbed the sweat off her neck. "I haven't made a punishment system yet. I didn't think we'd need one so soon."

"What would they be punished for?" Dot finally stopped, taking a break for water from one of her successful mugs.

"For killing the river creature." Olivia could not tell where this was going. Dot almost seemed like she was siding with them.

"Did you give everyone a rule about not killing river creatures?"

"Not explicitly, but it's right there in the main rule."

"The interpretation is a little vague. It could mean many different things." Dot shrugged and returned to work.

"Fine, it could mean other things, but everyone here knows what it implies, and Jeff went against it on purpose."

"How do you know?"

"It's the kind of person he is. Awful."

"Is your personal bias speaking? Or, maybe now you can read minds?"

"I can't read minds, feel emotion, or any of the other senses. I just know he's messing with me on purpose."

"Perhaps."

"Why else would he stay in this community?"

"Good question."

Dot might refuse to judge Jeff and Dave, but Olivia recognized them as a barrier to the dream she was trying to build. They should be punished, but she could do nothing this time. Dot was correct as usual. The rules were not firm enough.

Although, maybe justice could still be done. It was a windy afternoon and would likely be a windy night. If she removed the stakes from Jeff's tent after he fell asleep, the tent should only take an hour or less to come loose and collapse on him while he slept. Bonus points if they got another monsoon rain tonight.

Olivia's lips twisted into a smile as she made her after dark plans. Her minor revenge could come back to haunt her, but she preferred to think of it as giving karma an assisting hand. Rather like assigning Jeff all the afternoon tasks to make his sunburn worse.

Maybe if she made life difficult for the annoying old man, Jeff would take himself and his toady off to the bigger village and leave Olivia in peace.

"I'm going to take a personal break out in the forest. If you know what I mean." Olivia gestured vaguely toward the trees away from the building site.

"Take your time. Your mud will be waiting for your return," said Dot.

Olivia sighed inwardly and padded into the forest, trying to get out of hearing range of their workspace.

She wondered where Scott was disappearing off to these days. He was supposed to help this afternoon, but had begged off. Saying he needed some free time, and he'd join them at the building site tomorrow. Olivia didn't mind. She enjoyed the time alone with Dot. She always learned so much.

A snapping sound alerted her to a Biting Nettle. The snapping jaws of the plate-sized flower often wove into her dreams, and she was careful in the forest, watching for the things. They were hard to miss once you knew to look for them.

She had been considering breaking her own rule to eradicate them from the community area and surroundings. It would not be like she was on a crusade to kill all of them, right? With a mental forehead slap, she agreed with Dot. Her Harm None rule was too vague. For sure, don't harm humans and the Blue Kin. What about other lizards? Or birds? Where did it draw the line for plants? Chopping down the nettles? Was pulling up root vegetables or picking river plants for salad considered harm? Where did it stop?

She sighed aloud this time. She was going to have to create a legal system, something she'd hoped to avoid. With punishments she didn't even want to carry out.

With a head full of ideas, she always thought she'd be great in some role to make change happen, but maybe leadership was not her skill.

Realizing she'd wandered further than she'd meant to in her mental meanderings, she found a tall enough bush next to a tree and did her business quickly.

On the way back, she was shocked to see one of the newcomers reaching for one of the scary plant's berries.

"No!" she shouted. Knowing it was probably already too late.

The boy had grasped a berry, and at the gentlest tug of the plant, it sprang into action, attacking with speed and biting the boy's upper arm through his shirt.

Olivia was still racing over to help, even though she knew the boy was dead and he didn't know it yet. She reached out a hand. "Let me help you up."

The boy took her hand and stood, then saw her necklace. Eyes wide, the new arrival pushed Olivia back, saying, "I know who you are. I've already heard about you, and I don't want your help."

Olivia, landing dangerously close to the still aggravated nettle, dropped and rolled out of the way. Hearing the clacking behind her, she braced to feel the stabbing pain of a bite at any moment.

She stopped rolling when she was sure the plant could not stretch to reach her and flipped onto her back, splayed out on the soft ground cover plants to catch her breath. What a mess. Could things get any worse?

CHAPTER 11

Jeff

Jeff sat in his tent alone through the afternoon. Dave was away to gather more vines, and Jeff was supposed to be weaving them into the mats required for the new hut they were building. He knew if he didn't do the work, Dave would get it done eventually.

Instead, Jeff let his mind wander, dreaming of new ideas on how to take over the community. He rubbed his hands together. Everything was going perfectly. He'd talked the entire group of today's ten newcomers into heading to the bigger town. Same decision as the last group.

It would be less help for Olivia and would add more people to pay him taxes when he ruled the bigger village one day.

He and Dave had tried to meet the shuttle to get a better hold over them, but Olivia always ordered them to do other tasks while she took shuttle duty. No matter, she could not be around newcomers all the time. Jeff found plenty of ways to chat with them and sway them away from Olivia.

His freshest lie only worked on the newest and weak-minded, but it was his favorite so far. He'd been having Dave tell people how the girl meeting them at the shuttle, the one wearing the elaborate necklace, likes to murder newcomers in the forest. With everything so new here, even those who didn't believe were anxious enough to want to move to civilization rather than keep camping here.

One of the stupidest new arrivals Jeff had met so far rushed into his tent and sat next to him like they were friends.

"Can I assist you," said Jeff. His words were polite, but his lip cured and nose wrinkled at this repellent and sweaty, panicked boy.

"Is Alan here? He said I could come to him for help. I was trying to find food in the forest, and I was bitten by this big plant thing, and I was attacked by the crazy murdering girl Dave told me about. I barely escaped alive. I need to talk to Alan. I need to find some food. I don't feel well. It's probably hunger, the food bars are gross, but I need to eat. I'm so hungry."

Alan strolled in and heard the last comment. "Hey dude, no need to go hungry. I happen to have some tasty greens with me. I was bringing them for Jeff's dinner salad, but I have plenty to go around. They are sweet when you chew on them."

Jeff's mind was buzzing with the opportunity before him. He just had to line up all the facts, and he knew he only had minutes to do so.

This guy must have been bitten by a nettle since they had not found any other biting plants. The new boy had minutes to live, and nothing could save him. The sweet water plants brought by Alan had a deadly lookalike. If he could convince Alan he'd killed the boy, would it be enough to make him Jeff's willing servant again?

He needed to start getting the pieces in place. Reaching out for a stalk of the sweet plant, making sure it was after the new arrival had greedily downed several, he narrowed his eyes and said, "Alan, where did you get this plant."

"Across the river and upstream is a big patch I found on a long walk today."

So, the plant has not come from any of the usual spots, perfect. "You know, this plant looks strange. Are you sure it's not the poisonous lookalike?" Jeff widened his eyes as big as he could and stared at the newcomer.

At that moment, the boy tipped over sideways, dead.

The timing could not have been better. Instead of wondering why the plant poison worked so fast or considering any other possibilities, Alan fell to his knees and propped up the boy's head. Trying to shake him awake first and then feeling for a pulse.

"You killed him," said Jeff, trying to push as much shock as he could into the tone.

"No! I was sure those were right." Alan swallowed hard a couple of times. "I need to get him to a doctor." Alan swung the boy over his back and ran as fast as the load would let him. He had not even cleared the door when he remembered. "The doctor, he went with the others, to the big village."

"Yes, and it doesn't matter anyway. The boy is dead. Put him down outside."

While Alan was busy, Jeff gathered all the food plants, wrapped them inside one of the finished mats, and hid them under the new vines. He could not have Alan looking closely at them.

Alan returned, and Jeff had never seen him so disoriented. "I've hidden the poison plants. No one has to know you killed him. I'll protect you from Olivia. I'll do all the talking for you and say the boy found and ate some poisonous plants."

Alan didn't say anything. Shoulders hunched, tears in his eyes.

"No one has to know you killed him," Jeff repeated, using his kind voice, the one he used for interns on their first day before he broke their spirit later. It was even better if he could buddy up to them and find dirt he could hold over them. Like now, and what amazing gossip this was! Alan had killed someone and would be indebted to Jeff for getting him out of trouble.

Alan didn't know it yet, but the boy would be little more than a slave to Jeff after this moment.

"Go spend the afternoon out in the forest, getting your mind back on track, and report to me for dinner. Dave and I have some plans to work on, and we'll need your help."

Alan nodded and stumbled away.

Happiness streaked through Jeff. These were the kinds of lucky things that happened to him. He was always in the right place at the right moment to advance his career and personal power, no matter who he had to step on or kill. Even better if they killed themselves and saved him the trouble.

Although, he still had a dead boy outside his tent.

Jeff stood and shuffled outside. Alan had dropped the body, nearly blocking the tent doorway. Jeff sighed and kicked the boy's legs out his way.

Usually, he tried not to talk to Olivia or any of her friends and crew. He sent Dave to do the talking, or Alan, but he needed to handle this himself. He was pleased to find Olivia tending a fire outside her tent, keeping him from searching for the annoying girl.

"Hello Jeff, what do you need?" Olivia's jaw clenched, and she didn't meet his eyes.

"A stupid guy ate something wrong and died next to my tent. Remove the body."

Olivia replied, "Fine, I'll take care of it."

Jeff shrugged. The elaborate multi-layered speech he had prepared on the way over was not needed. Easier was better. Less lies to remember for later. However, he could always lie about having lied. It was surprisingly effective.

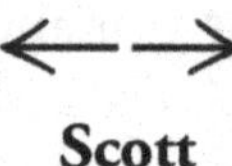

Scott

Scott had spent the last hour making the ruin they'd been meeting in - their spot - more comfortable. He'd started with some spare sleeping mats from people who had died, but the ground was too lumpy. So, he'd tried some grass mats under those, but it didn't help enough. What kind of past civilization didn't need a flat place to rest?

Finally, he'd borrowed some of the mud dug for the clay huts and used it to smooth out the uneven floor. Putting woven mats over the dirt, with doubled sleeping mats over those, it was finally comfy. Some old clothes covering a discarded tent tarp made a good pillow.

He was glad Alan was planning on being late. Preparations had all taken him longer than planned. He laid down on the mat, wondering if he could get a quick nap in, when he heard noises coming from the doorway.

During a conversation with Dot yesterday, Scott asked her to stay away from this one ruin for the foreseeable future. With a knowing smile, the old lady had promised she would not show that particular ruin to anyone else.

Confident in the knowledge only Dot knew this place was here and would not interrupt, he called quietly, "Hey cutie, I've got the place spruced up."

Alan came into view. His face red, eyes puffy from crying, breathing shallow and rapid.

"What's happened?"

Alan tried to speak, but only noises came out, squeaky and intelligible.

"Stop, stop. Don't talk. It looks like you are having a panic attack. Come sit down."

Getting Alan settled, he made him sip some water, then held both his hands and said, "Breathe. Breathe with me." He took in a deep breath and saw Alan try to follow his lead. A few breaths in, and he seemed calmer. A few breaths after that, and Alan's shoulders sagged weakly.

Scott gathered Alan in his arms and lay down. Putting his head on the hard pillow and letting Alan use his chest and shoulder to sob into.

What could have happened? What could have gone so wrong? He hoped Olivia and Finn were okay, and Dot. He would not shed tears over Jeff, but would be sad if some of the other elders had perished somehow.

He stroked Alan's hair, whispering it would be okay, and hoped it would be. Scott was lost on how else he could help.

When Alan was done crying, he sat up to drink more water and laid next to Scott again, using the same hard pillow so they could look at each other.

"Tell me what happened."

"I can't."

"You can."

"You'll hate me."

"Never."

Alan took a shaky breath. "I killed a man."

Scott reeled, but he didn't let it show. There must be an explanation. First, he could not imagine his sweet friend going around murdering people, and second, Alan would not be so upset if it was on purpose. "Tell me about it."

"It was an accident," said Alan.

"I knew it would be," replied Scott.

"How could you know?"

"Because I know you. Now, give me details."

"Do you remember the water plants we found on our walk this morning? The round ones? In the third patch we stopped at?"

"Kind of. I'm not a plant person."

"I got the wrong ones. I gave them to a newcomer, and he died. The boy died in front of me. It's all my fault. I killed him."

"Wait. Back up. How do you know it was the wrong plant?"

"Jeff told me."

"Jeff? How is he involved."

"This all happened in his tent. He told me I got the wrong plants. The boy died."

"That's convenient. Are you sure Jeff didn't kill him?"

"No. It was me. I fed him the plants. I watched him eat them. I watched him die."

Scott was not sure how any of the poisons worked. He had not assisted the doc or known anyone who died. It could be possible.

"Jeff said he would cover for me and take care of everything, but he wants me to come to another planning meeting tonight. I wasn't going to attend any more of those, but now, I guess I have to. Jeff is a good friend to make sure I don't get in trouble."

Scott had his doubts about Jeff's friendly intentions, but kept them to himself. Alan was finally coming back around to normal, and he didn't want to argue over the unimportant man.

He had to try one more time, though. "You have such a keen eye for plant harvest. It's one of your specialties. Are you sure you got the wrong plant?"

"I must have got the wrong plant. The boy died."

Scott frowned, but let it go. "Come here. It's been a long day and you've been through a lot. Let's take a nap, and everything will make more sense when we wake up."

Alan cuddled close, using Scott's chest as a pillow again for their afternoon rest.

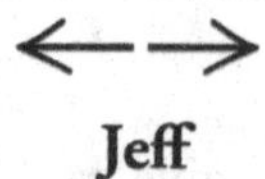

Jeff

The smell of charred meat hung in the air, refusing to dissipate in the stale mugginess with the doorway blocked for their secret meeting. Dave had presented the platter full of roasted lizards to an enthusiastic Jeff.

Finally, something Jeff could sink his teeth into instead of the rabbit food he'd been forced to eat so far.

As he ripped into another lizard, he glanced over at his co-conspirators. Dave appeared bland as he always did these days, but Alan looked like he would be sick. Either from watching the lizards be eaten or from the plans they'd discussed so far. Jeff didn't care which it was, the boy was his now, but he should make it clear why he planned to sabotage Main Camp.

"Alan, do you know why we stayed with this group of savages?"

Alan shrugged. He'd been refusing to speak all night.

"Even though we could become a member of the other communities with trading or money, I don't want to be a member. I will be the ruler. I know we can be in charge of the whole planet and have power over all the communities. You could rule at my side. Doesn't that sound like a good future?"

Alan shrugged again, his shoulders returning to a deep droop, and began twisting the grass from his skirt around his finger and then off. On and off. On and off.

Jeff, momentarily mesmerized by the repetitive motion, snapped, "Stop it."

Alan jumped.

"Won't you eat something? You must be hungry." Jeff pushed the plate of blackened lizards toward Alan. Smiling when he saw the boy cringe and swallow hard a couple of times before shaking his head.

"If we can get control of Main Camp, we'll be in the position Olivia wants for herself. To influence the newcomers and control trade with the other villages."

Alan tried to speak, but it came out squeaky. He cleared his throat and said his first words of the meeting. "Well, I don't think that's what Olivia is doing."

In quick defense of their leader, Dave said, "Of course, it's what she's doing. Don't contradict Jeff."

Jeff gave Dave a pleased smile and continued his lecture. "We don't want to go to the places with money yet, because we'd all have to get a job and work. I could get a lot more done by being the person in charge. I can help these failing fools by providing a unified government."

Dave chimed in with an enthusiastic, "Exactly!"

Jeff clapped his hands, clasping them together and resting his chin on them. "We must be in charge of the Main Camp because this is the seat of power. All we need to do is put tonight's plans in place to get us started."

Alan spoke again, with the boldness to disagree a second time. "I don't think this is a good idea. I don't want to help with this. I have not minded being your message runner to coordinate meetings or bring you extra greens for your meals, but this feels wrong."

"No, you must help me," said Jeff, pinning Alan with a steady gaze, "Like I helped you."

Alan looked down, and Jeff grinned. "The three of us working together can bring Olivia down."

"Exactly!" Dave said.

"After we gain control of Main Camp, believe me, we'll make our dreams into reality."

Dave grinned. "Why be a peasant when you can be a ruler."

"Exactly," agreed Jeff.

CHAPTER 12

Olivia

Olivia glared at the empty food hut, hands on hips and stomach churning. Constantly on edge, she was spending more time angry than happy these days, even fake happy. "I can't imagine where the food is going. This is the third day in a row."

"Could it perhaps be eaten? Maybe by Puddles?" Finn suggested hesitantly.

"Puddles takes a single large fruit a day, and I'm happy to share with him. This room has been cleared out!" Olivia waved her arms wildly at the empty baskets as she circled the interior of the hut.

"Well, don't shout at me. I didn't eat all the food." Finn carefully stepped over Scott's legs to leave the hut and stomped away.

Scott sitting by the entrance, using the wall to lean against, said, "We'll need to gather more. Do you want me to sit here and guard the food tomorrow?"

"I would, but it will take all of us to gather more, especially since we'll need to travel even further to forage. These forests have been stripped when everyone was still camping here, and after having to restock the last two days, we have hardly any food left to harvest."

"At least the new arrivals from yesterday have their food bars. Same with the next group."

"True, but I wanted to welcome them by showing off the tasty bounty of this planet. Not force them to run through their rations." Olivia covered her eyes and shook her head. "Jeff is behind this, him and his friends. I'm sure of it."

Scott crossed his arms and leaned his head back against the wall, staring at the cloudless sky. "Perhaps."

Olivia slapped her forehead with one hand, saying, "Who else could it be?"

Scott shrugged.

Olivia deflated, letting out a big breath. She also carefully stepped over Scott's legs, still blocking the entrance. "On second thought, you should stay here. I'll gather all the spare food and bring it back, and you guard it. I'll put everyone else on foraging duty, so we'll have food for dinner and breakfast at least."

A slight glint returned to Olivia's eyes. "I know this was Jeff's doing."

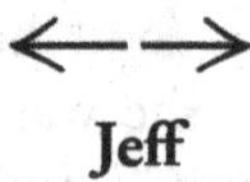

Jeff

Jeff stretched out on his mat, his feet and arms sore from another long walk to hide the food they'd stolen in the early morning. Luckily, he had the afternoon off from chores and planned to take a nap.

"Message!" came the call from outside his tent.

"Come in." Jeff sat with a big yawn.

He didn't recognize the girl. She must be one of the new arrivals from yesterday's shuttle drop.

"I was asked to tell you, because of a temporary food shortage, you need to gather Dave and Alan to harvest tree fruits upstream next to the big rock because it's one of the only places left with food. Oh, and the tools are not available for your team, also because of the food shortage."

Fury sprang into Jeff's chest and spurred him to his feet as quickly as his stiff old bones could move. "The big rock area is crawling with Biting Nettles, and it's impossible to harvest the trees without tools."

The girl frowned and backed up a step. "I don't know anything about it. I just volunteered to bring you the message," she said, running back outside.

Instead of pacing in his tent alone, he left to go pace in Dave's tent.

"Dave! There was just a messenger."

Dave raised his hand and cut him off. "I heard."

"We can't go to the big rock. We'll die."

"I'm not going."

"What?"

"We're elders in this community, and these kinds of chores are too taxing. I doubt Dot is being made to run around and harvest."

Jeff paused midstep. "Yeah."

"Besides, I'm not going to go gather fruit that we'll steal again tomorrow. I'd be creating more work for myself."

Jeff decided he must be too tired. Why did he think of this? It was clever of him to pick a good assistant.

Dave returned his attention to this weaving. "Go lay down and finish your nap, sir. You'll feel more yourself after a nice rest."

Jeff nodded, and ambled off, grumbling, "Pointless messengers."

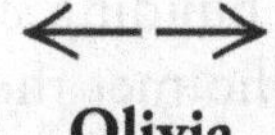

Olivia

"Hey, you!" Olivia ran to a new arrival dragging a tent tarp full of mud. "Where are you going?"

"I was told to take this mud to the build site." The young boy, one of the youngest Olivia had seen here, had his arms crossed, ready for an argument.

What could have caused such a hostile attitude? "The build site is the other direction." Olivia pointed back to camp, waving at the trees beyond.

"I was told to take it this direction." The boy remained stubbornly in place. His chin raised slightly.

"Who told you to bring it this way?"

"The girl with the black ponytail."

"Okay, well, she was wrong. I need this mud over there."

"No."

"What?"

"I was already given my instructions, and I don't have to take orders from you." The boy grasped the edges of the tarp and continued dragging in the wrong direction.

"I am the leader here."

"No, you're not. You are just an imposter. Leave me alone."

Speechless, Olivia did as the boy asked, leaving him alone.

She found the new arrival with the black ponytail by the cook fires. "Did you deliver a message about a load of mud?"

The girl twisted a ring on her finger nervously and put the fire between her and Olivia before saying. "Yes."

"What was the message," Olivia demanded.

"It was, um, well." The girl twisted the ring on her finger faster, her eyes darting around, looking for help.

Anger rippled through Olivia. She tried not to shout, but said again, "What was the message?"

"I was asked to tell the first three strong boys I could find there were loads of clay to be taken to the building site at the big rock in the distance. To also tell them, if the girl who met them at the shuttle objected to the location, to ignore her because she's trying to take over as the leader?"

Heat crept up Olivia's face. Rage searing through her brain. "Who gave you the message?"

"I don't know his name. He had curly dark hair."

Alan.

Olivia would tear apart the camp to find the troublemaker. Even though she had no doubt it was done on Jeff's orders. First, she had people to save.

Bursting into Finn's tent without calling out, she found him studying the native language guide.

"Hey! Excuse me. The rule is to call out."

"I didn't have time."

"What if I was naked?"

"This is an emergency."

Finn leaped to his feet in one smooth move, irritation replaced by alarm, shouting, "You should have led with that. What's wrong?"

"We have three new arrivals from today heading toward the big rock, and I have not briefed them on the Biting Nettle yet."

"What? Why?"

"I don't have time to explain. Can you gather a few people and go after them? Take the girl by the cookfire. She sent them out there."

"Why? And why can't you go?"

"I don't have time to explain. Just hurry."

Finn dashed past her, calling to Dot and the girl by the fire.

Olivia's temporarily pushed aside fury returned in a flood, and she prowled the camp searching for Alan.

While she searched, she formed all the things she'd say to the boy. How he had put people in danger, undermined Olivia's leadership, created double work.

Everything fled her mind when she found Alan.

In a meadow flooded with light and short wildflowers was Alan, with Scott. Both laying on their sides heads propped on elbows close enough they could have been kissing. They were whispering, and Scott had a happy, contented grin she'd never seen before on her friend's face.

She wished Finn was this close to her, but shoved the thought away as irrelevant.

Alan kissed Scott's forehead before hopping up and waving goodbye.

Olivia was undecided on what to do next. Should she go after Alan and give him the verbal beating he deserved? Her anger with Alan warred with the thrill of seeing her friend so happy.

Deciding to leave it for now and hash it out with Alan later, she took a step forward into the meadow. Smiling at her friend spread eagle among the flowers.

"Hi, Olivia." Scott still had a dreamy expression and a happy tone.

"Is there a reason you're cavorting with the enemy?" Olivia meant to sound teasing, but all the frustration from the situation seeped into her words. She cringed at the judgment she heard from herself.

"Alan is not the enemy. We don't have any enemies."

"What are you talking about? Jeff is actively trying to hinder the creation of this community."

"He's just pulling pranks. Don't think I haven't noticed you doing the same to him."

"People could have died today."

Scott sighed. All his happiness fled, replaced with the sad, worried boy Olivia knew. "Leave me alone," he said.

"It's the second time today someone has told me that."

"Maybe you should listen. Go away, Olivia."

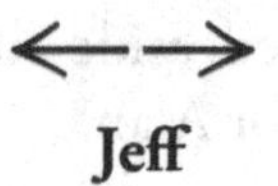

Jeff

"I'm too important for trash duty." Jeff's fuming didn't make the task go any faster, but it made him feel better. "Besides, it's against her own community rules to assign us the same task all week."

"It's because we refused to forage," pointed out Dave. He scraped another bit of dirt out of the hole using the palm-sized fruit shell and placed the soil to the side.

A row of filled-in holes stretched to the left of him, showing each day they buried their trash out here at the edge of the camp.

Jeff was supposed to be down there on his knees digging with Alan and Dave, but he paced and shouted. His knees could not take the pressure, and the elders should not be required. This was work for younger men.

When he'd pointed that out, Olivia replied all the younger boys and girls were leaving for the bigger towns based on things Jeff told them. It was wholly true, but he was stunned Olivia was smart enough to have caught on so soon after only three groups departed. He'd keep going with the lies, but he needed something more. Both to take over the camp and get back at Olivia for this week's labor.

"Alan! Why haven't you stolen the food the last few days? Dave and I wait in my tent, and you don't bring us anything. In fact, you don't come back at all!"

"A guard is posted on the hut now."

Alan's little smile about this comment infuriated Jeff. He was tired of Alan's laziness, always dragging his feet and protesting Jeff's good ideas. Worse, Alan had set down his shell tool and was playing with the grass. "What are you fiddling with?"

Alan blew out a big sigh. "I'm just moving a lizard out of the way."

"What? It's even slower than you are?" Jeff smiled smugly as Dave snorted a laugh at the taunt.

"These lizards move slow, hardly at all." Alan, finished with his rescue, returned to his digging. Jeff didn't like Alan's tone. It sounded disrespectful, but this sparked an idea for him.

"Do you think you could gather some of those slow lizards?"

"I suppose so. Why?" Alan finally glanced at Jeff, his eyes narrowed. Reluctance etched into early worry lines of his young face.

Jeff didn't bother answering Alan's questions, asking, "How many could you gather?"

Olivia

"You sent a runner for me?" Finn stepped into Olivia's tent

"Look at this mess."

Finn's initial chuckle turned into a belly laugh as he took in the lizards. Clinging to her ongoing projects, personal baskets of fruits, hanging from tent poles, surrounding her bed area, and clustered all over her spare clothing.

Finn's laughter had trailed off, but he cracked himself up again when he asked, "Starting a collection?"

Olivia didn't see anything funny about this. "The whole camp is overrun with them. You didn't have any in your tent?" she demanded.

"A few. Not this many." His response sent him into peals of laughter again.

Probably he found the situation humorous, but it felt like he was laughing at her.

"I'm sure Jeff is involved, and Alan too."

"Maybe they migrate," suggested Finn.

Olivia ground her teeth, but could not keep in her feelings. "That is the stupidest thing I've ever heard."

Finn's laughter stopped. The smile wiped from his face. "You're the stupidest thing I've ever seen," he shouted as he stomped out of the tent.

"Fine, run away again!" she shouted after him.

Olivia collapsed in the middle of her tent. The delicate lizards were slow and small, but some of the larger ones were aggressive and trying to bite. Clearly, they were not in the mood for being moved again. When she managed to get two hands free, the other two hands and the tail would still cling. It was hopeless. She was just going to have to live with them now.

She'd called Finn for help, hoping they could have a quiet moment together, and even that had gone sideways.

Olivia walked into the forest. Apparently, she was in no shape to handle animals or talk to people. So, she'd just get far away.

Past the half-finished cob house and past the clacking Biting Nettle, the one she was still trying to decide if she should kill. Past a dense grove of trees, she thought she heard a laugh and an accompanying giggle, but did not see anyone near.

She kept walking.

Maybe this was the day she'd get all the way to the headland. Perhaps she'd go past it and never return to camp. No one wanted her here.

In the near distance, she heard a repetitive shaking sound, like a rattlesnake, but with a high-pitched buzz at the end. Warily tracking the noise deeper into the woods, she came across a large tree she'd never seen before, its leaves puffy like cotton, and its bark covered in finger-length beetles.

They crawled over every branch and each other, some flying in the air, some dropping from the branches above. A few landed on her arms. She worried they might be dangerous, but so far, none of the bugs here bothered to bite any of the humans, and these were no exception.

The terrible ear-splitting sound they were emitting was overwhelming and made Olivia want to run in any direction they were not. She was glad the camp was far away. These would keep her up all night or drive her mad, or both.

An idea rolled into Olivia's head, and she laughed out loud. Feeling lighter than she had in days, she took out a spare pouch tied to her skirt and shook a few of the beetles into it, saying, "I know just what to do with these."

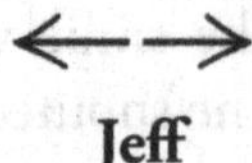

Jeff

"Do you hear that? It started up again!" Jeff sat on his mat, trying to see into every corner of the new grass hut he shared with Dave.

"Of course, I hear it," moaned Dave. "You'd have to be dead not to hear it."

"It's been two days now. It's not going away. I've checked with others, and their grass hut didn't come with this noise."

Dave held his hands over his ears, eyes wild. "We should have known better than to accept Olivia's help when she offered for all the villagers to come together for the construction phase of the hut."

"She does it for all the huts."

"Yes, but why would she do it for you?"

"The noise must be hidden. Somewhere in the joints, or the roof! Help me look."

"I'll do it tomorrow."

"You aren't getting any sleep. Get up. Now."

Dave obeyed, stumbling upright, rubbing his eyes, and yawning.

At first, the sound seemed to come from everywhere in the hut, but with carefully measured steps, they pinpointed the corner closest to Jeff's mat. Feeling along the seam, Jeff found a bump near the top and pulled down a pouch.

Inside the pouch, hideous strange bugs continued making the horrible noise.

"Isn't that one of the pouches Olivia carries everywhere with her?"

Jeff vibrated with rage at the two nights of lost sleep. Closing the bag, he threw it on the ground. After putting his shoes on, he repeatedly stomped on the paper pouch until peaceful silence returned.

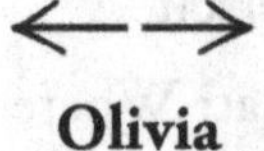

Olivia

Olivia was sore everywhere. The cob house was taking shape, but it required every muscle to continue working the sandy mud with her legs and stretch her arms to mold it into the high walls.

She wanted to beg off other chores, but it wouldn't be fair. So, she sat by the cook fire, slowly building it higher to make dinner of cooked greens and jam, her new favorite these days.

"Hi Finn, are you on cooking duty tonight?" Olivia tried to smile, but exhaustion showed through.

"Why are you going to fight Jeff? Isn't your childish feud bad enough?"

"Fight Jeff? What?"

"You challenged him to a fight! In the meadow tomorrow! How could you? It's completely unnecessary and irresponsible." Finn crossed his arms and glared at Olivia.

A laugh burst out of she. "Of all the ridiculous nonsense. I don't even know how to fight."

"So, you didn't challenge Jeff to a duel?"

"No. Even if it was true. What do you care if I die tomorrow?"

"I do care. I don't know what's going on these days, but I believe in the vision you shared with me. I'm starting to think it will never work, but I'd like to try before giving up and heading to civilization. If you died, the vision would die with you."

"Great, so you only need me around for my ideas."

"Why are you being so difficult?"

"Same to you. Hey, where are you going? Aren't you on cooking duty?"

Olivia watched Finn's retreating form. She thought she had longer to chat with him. Oh, well. She'd probably just make things worse anyway.

Adding more driftwood to the fire, she realized they would need to start using trees or stop having fires soon.

In the midst of this depressing thought, she saw Scott swerving toward her on the way to the fruit hut, full baskets in his hands. "Hey, there's a rumor going around about the leader, that's you. It's said she stole all the food, and she's hiding it for herself."

"How could you believe that? Where would I even put all the food?"

"I don't believe it, silly girl. I just thought I'd let you know." Scott shifted his grip on the baskets and continued walking, giving Olivia an eye roll.

The fire was finally finished, and Olivia was too tired to shift away when Dot sat next to her. "Heard the one about the bands of raiders?"

Olivia frowned. "The what?"

"It's a story flying through the camp like wildfire. Apparently, some of the groups of ten dropped off by the shuttle formed warring tribes that raid this camp. Often."

"Who would believe such nonsense?"

"Not many, but these rumors are not sitting easy with today's newcomers. All ten are anxious to all leave first thing in the morning."

"This is frustrating. I was sure some of the new arrivals would eventually stay here in Main Camp instead of heading off to Blue Valley."

"Maybe it's a naming thing. Main Camp sounds temporary. Blue Valley sounds enchanting. With the bonus of the promise of civilization. Something you are not even pretending you'll provide."

"We have something better here."

"Do we? I'm half tempted to head over to Blue Valley myself. Things are not going well for you."

"Fine! Leave! You, and Finn, and anyone else who doesn't like my village can escape to a paycheck and a boring life."

Disconcerted to find herself crying, Olivia ran to the beach to spend some quiet time sitting with the Blue Kin.

CHAPTER 13

Jeff

Jeff watched Alan shuffle in, carrying a basket with a lid. "You're late."

Alan sat as close to the doorway as possible. Setting the basket next to him and staring sullenly into his hands.

Jeff was having a harder and harder time controlling the boy these days. Maybe he needed to put his foot down. "What's in the basket?"

"A project."

"I asked what's in it, loser."

Alan gazed out the open doorway, refusing to acknowledge the comment.

Jeff had two options. He could change topics or take the basket by force. Alan was a lot younger, so he went with the first option.

"Last night, Dave changed the bathroom direction trail markers - since you refused to - and several people were lost in the forest all night."

"I still think it was dangerous." Alan pointed out.

Jeff smiled widely, so his teeth showed. "Not only is there unrest because of what happened, Olivia publicly blamed Scott for doing it wrong, saying the boy is always lost in a daydream." Jeff could not hold in gleeful laughter at this turn of events. Olivia was losing allies fast. If anything, Olivia was doing more to help their plans along than Alan.

Dave set aside the skirt he was working on, taking a short break to gossip. "The accusation has not gone over well with anyone. Scott is well-loved by all."

"It's too perfect. Almost as fun as the rumors. I wonder if we could spread a rumor after the next shuttle drop, something about how Olivia only took over main camp because she's planning to murder all the newcomers?"

"That one is a bit much and probably won't be believed as easily," said Dave.

"Besides, isn't it going too far?" asked Alan unhappily.

Irritation swelled in Jeff's chest. This attitude was beyond unacceptable. Alan was questioning every word out of his mouth. "You'd know about too far. Remember, you killed a boy!" snapped Jeff.

Watching for the respect to return, Jeff was startled when Alan's jaw dropped and he left with a word.

Only then did Jeff remember Dave knew nothing about the hold he'd gained over Alan. He darted a look at his only ally. Dave's eyes were narrowed in deep thought, but otherwise remained calm and focused on his handwork.

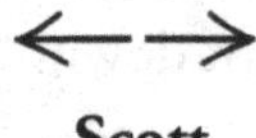

Scott

Scott waited in their spot, examining the glowing mushrooms and wondering if they could be moved and replanted. They would be amazing in the cob houses Dot planned to build.

When Alan arrived, it was clear he was angry. He paced the small room, breathing short and quick, his hands swinging wildly as he muttered to himself.

"What's wrong?" asked Scott.

"I don't even know where to start."

Scott took Alan's trembling hands and led him to the mat. Sitting cross-legged in front of Alan, he said, "Start at the beginning."

"It's such a mess. There are several beginnings." Alan sat cross-legged too, so their knees were touching, and clasped his hands in his lap, staring at the intertwined fingers.

Scott put his hands over Alan's. "Start at the oldest beginning and work your way to today."

Alan met Scott's reassuring gaze with a nervous smile. "Okay. I can do that." After a steadying breath, Alan began. "I didn't tell you when it happened, but I got my sixth sense. I thought I would not get one because everyone seemed to have one except me, and even after I could sense things, I could not figure out what I was sensing. Felt like it arrived late and broken. About a week ago, I figured it out."

Alan paused, smiling shyly. Scott reached out and shook the other boy's knees lightly. "Don't leave me in suspense. What is it?"

"I can sense lies. It took me time to figure it all out, but I've been sure for days now."

"Good thing I speak my mind."

"Actually, it is a good thing. Before now, I had no idea how often people lie. White lies, social lies, actual lies, hurtful lies." Alan trailed off, clasping his hands and retreating into sadness again.

Scott lifted Alan's chin with one hand and kissed him, a quick hard kiss on the lips. "Your new skill is cool, thanks for telling me about it, but what has you upset?"

"When Jeff told me I killed a boy. It tore me up. I was responsible for ending the whole life of a person. It was a lot to handle and I have not felt like myself. Since then, Jeff has been holding it over me, making me do things."

Scott held in any impatience, keeping it out of his tone as he said, "I know you've pushed back and helped where you can."

"So have you. All that time guarding the fruit hut, so I had an excuse not to steal any more food. Creating the pretend build site, so no one would get anywhere near the big rock with the nettles. Helping me collect lizards and listening to me whine. Without you, I could not have made it through."

"I still think you should have just told Olivia it was an accident and stayed away from Jeff, but I'm proud of you for doing what you could."

"I was ashamed. People would know I'd messed up the foraging."

"I still can't imagine how it happened. You are too good."

"I am too good. I didn't kill him."

"What? How do you know?"

"Today, Jeff accused me again of killing the boy. It was the strongest lie I've ever felt. I don't know who killed that dude, but it wasn't me." Alan put a hand on his chest and took a deep breath. "It wasn't me."

Scott threw his arms around Alan in a big hug, and they fell over onto the mat together.

"I'm so dumb. Doing all those things Jeff wanted. I feel terrible about all the harm I've caused."

"What are you going to do about it?"

"What can I do?"

"Well, the information you've gained in Jeff's confidence has proved useful more than once. If you can stomach being around him, you might be able to warn us."

"Great! I'll be Alan, the Double Agent."

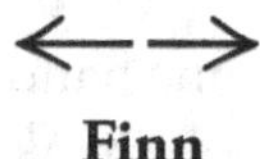

Finn

Finn missed books. On a day like this, with a summer breeze and plenty of shady spots, he'd be devouring a book a day if they were available. Instead, he was simply relaxing under a shady tree near camp when Olivia arrived back. She'd been gone for three days.

He didn't believe the rumor she'd fallen off a cliff, and yet, it was a relief to see her alive. "Olivia!" he called, waving her over.

She trudged toward him, her tent and everything she owned slung over a shoulder.

"So, you didn't keep all the lizards," he said with a grin.

"Nope, they didn't like me. No one does," Olivia said with a shrug as she sat across from him. Still in the shade, but a distance away. "How is your hand? Looks like the splint is off."

"It might be too soon to remove it, but I could not stand it anymore. My ribs are feeling better too."

"I'm glad."

"So, where have you been?"

"I needed to get away, to think."

"What did you think about?"

"I'm starting to wish I didn't put my name forward. Being one of the camp counselors under Dot was so different than being the sole leader."

"You have struggled."

"I don't think I'm cut out for this. I'm autistic, so along with a strong sense of justice spurring my war with Jeff, I always seem to say the worst possible thing to people. Especially to you." Her eyes, downcast up to this point, glanced at him and then quickly away.

"You do have an interesting way with words." Some of Olivia's words and actions made a little more sense with her revelation. Although, it didn't make much difference to him now that he could tell what she was feeling along with her words. These days, with his talent refined, often her meaning was sometimes clearer to him no matter what tone she used.

"I feel partly at fault for everything that went wrong here," continued Olivia. "Besides annoying people, I've been playing Jeff's game with him. I could have halted the obvious sabotage by simply sending him away."

"Yes. These petty tricks must stop if we are to succeed in becoming a real community."

"I'll talk to Jeff before we kick him out. I just have to figure out the words."

"You might not have to. Maybe Jeff is giving up. All ten people in the last drop are staying in this community."

"Great! We need more people for this village."

"It's a relief. Maybe things are finally looking up." Finn was glad they were talking again. He'd missed the conversation they'd had before the big vote. When Olivia had been content, if lonely, and they could actually talk openly. Since that day, she'd been so stressed they'd only managed to growl at each other.

"Your friend is in a hurry." Olivia pointed, and Finn saw Puddles running toward them in his most skittering run. He was used to seeing Puddles around camp these days, as often to visit him as to snack in the fruit tent.

He drew a greeting in the dirt in preparation for a possible chat, but when Puddles arrived, the lizard brushed it out and didn't return the greeting.

Finn sensed agitation and fear, noting his antennae were flat against his head. The lizard started to draw a symbol, but brushed it out. Tried again and brushed it out. His rising frustration evident, even without an emotional sense of him. Finn drew the symbol for slow.

Puddles whole body shivered, tip to tail. He carefully drew a symbol, followed by two more.

Finn frowned. "He says there's a rainstorm coming."

CHAPTER 14

Finn

Finn paused before stepping onto the beach. It seemed like a great idea to ask the older and wiser Blue Kin what Puddles was trying to warn them about, but the lizards were a hive of activity. Some piling sand and swishing it flat with their tails, others pacing or chattering with each other.

The guard closest to them was Storm, and Finn felt Olivia tense at recognizing the only Blue Kin to ever attack a human. With good reason, but still.

Trading occasional greetings or ideas with the natives, he had only ever had long conversations with Puddles, so he was pleased when talking to Storm was easier.

"Hello," he scratched into the sand, following it with symbols, one for each word or concept. "Puddles told me rain is coming."

"Yes. Rain over the ocean. Too much water."

"Rain on land too?" He was sure there was a better way to use the symbols and renewed his internal vow to find a better way to understand their language one day. If anyone could do it, he could, since he could feel what they meant instead of entirely relying on the writing.

He sensed Storm felt both scared and proud when he clarified, "Not only rain, a huge storm is coming. This is the Storm I am named for. Coming from the ocean, it will hit land hard."

Finn decided any storm this fierce this powerful guard was named for would not be easy to get through. It didn't give him comfort.

"Ocean water is moving, very dangerous, and the storm is coming soon. We are leaving Star Bay to hide. Come back again later. You hide far away too. Goodbye."

"Thank you. Goodbye." Finn carefully drew the symbols and backed away. Through the whole encounter, he had been finding words in the guidebook at a frantic pace to keep up with the more fluent Storm, but was pleased to note many of the words were familiar.

Finn watched the agitated lizards for a moment, then turned to Olivia. "I've never been in one, but do you know what the description sounds like?"

"Rain over the ocean? Are you thinking of a hurricane too?"

"Yep. We should warn Main Camp."

Most of the community of Main Camp chose to not believe. Finn could not understand why. A big storm was coming, and people said the Blue Kin were probably lying or easy to panic.

One of the women elders told Finn her sixth sense is for water, and she could feel a lot of water. Not as much as the ocean, just a similar feeling of the sea, but in the air.

Finn and the elder joined Olivia and Scott, with a few other people making preparation plans. Bundling gear that might blow away and stashing extra supplies in known ruins.

As the believers chatted and brainstormed, the wind picked up.

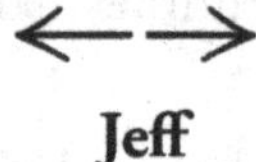

Jeff

"Those lizards are probably exaggerating. They are dumb animals, but we're not afraid of a little rain." Jeff leaned back and smiled his deal-winning smile at some of the group who had arrived only hours before. He'd invited them into his hut for a chat after their tents were pitched.

One of the newcomers glanced out of the hut opening, his eyes wide and hands twisting in his lap. "The sky is so overcast. Is it usually like this?"

Jeff flapped a hand and laughed confidently. "Oh sure, we get heavy rain sometimes. It keeps the forest green."

"What about the wind? I heard someone say this wind is unusually strong."

Jeff held back his annoyance and kept his public persona in place. "Well, a storm is coming, of course, it's simply not as bad as the native aliens say it is. They should not be trusted."

The group of five nodded and seemed reassured. Now that he'd gained their belief, it was time to start the next part of his plan. "The other person you can't trust is the girl you met at the shuttle. She says she's the leader for Main Camp, but she's weak. Weak on management and on crime."

"Is there crime?"

"Of course! She's failing as a leader, letting others make choices for her. A puppet being controlled. She can't really lead."

"Why is she the leader, then?"

"She was voted in by friends, but she could be replaced at any time with another community vote. I believe it's what must happen, and soon." Jeff met the eyes of everyone in the tent to show the importance of this statement.

"She also abuses her power. She put me on trash duty for a whole week even though she knows my old knees can't handle it. She yells at people when they make mistakes. Also, she says we keep losing all the harvested food, but she's hoarding it for herself. We need someone older, with more experience at leading. Like when I was the leader of many banks, I had to work up to the role. The girl is simply too young to lead a group this large. Believe me."

"Maybe you should lead the group. Since you have already done that job," said one of the new boys.

Jeff smiled and nodded as if the thought had never occurred to him. "Yeah, perhaps I could. We must find a new leader instead of the nut job. Nobody likes her. I'll only call the girl stupid because it's mean to call her a disgraced failure."

After Dave had ushered them all out, he came back and said, "Went well. Are you ready for the next half of the group?"

"Yeah. After dinner, start bringing in groups from the previous shuttle drop. It's time to show everyone how amazing I am. Olivia's leadership will be over soon."

Jeff watched Dave stride out into the rain, like it was a bright cloudless day. The rancher ignored both the water pelting down and the wind strong enough to sway the grass hut.

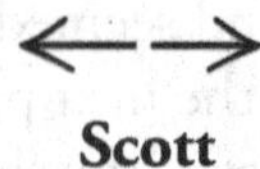

Scott

"This is bad, Alan."

Alan sat and watched Scott wandering aimlessly around and between the trees. Neither of them doing the chores they came together for. "The storm can't be too bad. It's probably typical if the lizards know about it, and the trees seem to survive okay."

"Have you been in a hurricane before?"

"No."

"I have. Several times. It's in the air, the wind, the persistent overcast sky, the building pressure, can't you feel it?"

Alan shrugged. "Maybe. Jeff is going around telling everyone it's no big deal and to not bother preparing."

"I noticed and I'm worried. Jeff's personality is so strong everyone believes in him."

"Like I used to believe in him?" Alan smiled wryly, and added, "Olivia will make sure everyone is safe. She has Dot to help her."

"That's just it. Jeff has been telling everyone the storm is not real and to ignore Olivia and Dot. I've gone around trying to convince them otherwise, but it's no use."

Alan shrugged again and patted the ground next to him. "It'll be okay."

Scott halted, changing course toward Alan and plopping down. "Are you able to sense your own lies?"

Alan laughed. "I'll just have to make it true."

Scott kissed him. "Thanks. For listening to my worries."

"Well, maybe we can do more than worry. How do you prepare for a hurricane?" Alan asked as he shifted closer to Scott.

"Fortify your shelter. Which we don't even have here!"

"We don't?" Alan was nuzzling his neck. Scott was sure it was meant as a distraction. Surprisingly effective.

"No, we don't have anything to fortify," he said, trying to stay on topic. "Tents and grass huts are hopeless."

"I'm not talking about tents or huts. What about the ruins? We don't have to share our little ruin, of course, but other ruins are scattered through the forest, right?"

"Yes! It could work. I'll talk to Dot about it," Scott said, finally surrendering to Alan's playful kisses.

CHAPTER 15

Finn

The rain stung Finn as he ran through the water-logged camp paths. After everyone else left, most people had stayed spread out instead of clumping together. Which forced him to slosh through the mud all the way to the other side of the meadow.

On arrival, he burst into the tent to get away from the worsening rain. "Come on, it's time to go!" he shouted over the wind.

"No way, we won't set foot in those creepy ruins just to avoid some heavy rain." The boy spoke for himself, and two other boys huddled together on the sleeping mats.

"I don't think these tents will hold up to this rain, and it's getting worse," said Finn. "You must come with me."

"No."

Finn was baffled. This was his last group to lead to the ruins, but not the first group that had refused to go with him. He shook his head, a quick frustrated shake flinging water into his eyes. With nothing else to do or say, he stomped out of the tent and back into the rain.

The rain was harder than before he'd spent a few minutes in the tent. The wind pushed against him, lashing rain into his eyes, so he could not tell where he was going. He kept his eyes down and tried to focus on the swiftly flooding path.

Reaching the forest, darker than usual from the heavily overcast sky, he followed the path deep into the trees where the rain calmed enough to let him view the surroundings.

Taking a few more steps forward to be sure, he discovered he'd gone completely the wrong way. Instead of inland, he was on the beach path.

The ocean in view from the thinning trees near the beach showed waves higher than he'd ever seen here. Fast and wild, the waves pounded up to the tree line.

The water mesmerized him for a moment, receding slightly, but coming back stronger and higher with each forward wave. He could not imagine where the Blue Kin had gone to stay safe. Perhaps inland, where he should be. Finn hoped Puddles was okay.

Turning away from the waves, he tried to figure out the best way to get to the ruins from here and was pushed from behind by a wall of water.

He saw a tree coming toward him, or he was headed toward the tree.

Too close! Too fast to stop.

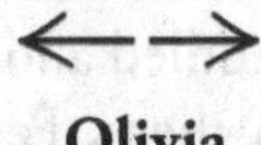

Olivia

The rain beat Olivia's head, shoulders, and chest. Awakening pain in bruises she thought were healed. The sound of the rain, so overwhelming she could barely think straight. Still feeling the burden of leadership, she went from tent to tent, trying to get people to follow her to the ruins.

She'd sent Finn after the last of the boys on the far meadow, hoping he could convince them when she could not. It appeared Scott was having more luck than she was. On the way to the ruins, past the last of the camp, she saw several people join Scott's group for evacuation.

Leading the six people with her through the forest was difficult. Early darkness had descended, and the paths in the lower part of the forest were already flooded. She kept wiping the rain from her eyes, wishing for a rain jacket with a hood.

They would be safe soon. Dot had found the largest ruin on high ground. Plenty of space for everyone, the gear, and food they'd stored from the few people who had planned ahead based on Puddle's and Finn's warning.

Finn. He floated into her mind like he often did. She'd sent him to gather a single group, three boys, so he'd be behind Scott, who was right behind her. They'd all be safe soon.

Olivia arrived at the ruins, sliding between the close-growing trees that often hid the entrances to these unnatural caves. Still leading the way, she burst into the tunnel first. The break from the noise of the wind and the feeling of the rain on her skin was a huge relief. She stood still and took several deep breaths.

The people bumping into her from behind forced her to move deeper down the sloping tunnel. In the room beyond, the smell hit her first. A group of terrified damp people. It almost made her want to go back out in the fresh rain, despite the potential hurricane.

Dot came over and peered past her after the six had descended and settled. "Good grief. Is this all? Where is everyone else?"

"Some refused to come. I don't understand it. Scott convinced a group, and Finn should be coming with more. They'll be here any moment." Olivia surveyed the room. It looked like most everyone was here or would be soon. Even Jeff and Dave huddled and chatted. Scheming probably. She noted Alan sat well apart from them. Perhaps Scott was right about Alan not being the enemy.

Scott stumbled down the ramp, leading ten people into the space.

Olivia rubbed her short hair, flicking the water in many directions. "Did you see Finn and his group of three? He should be behind you."

"Actually, I think I saw someone headed in the direction of the beach. Hard to tell in the distance and rain. It could have been Finn. I've been wondering if I should check." Scott squeezed more water out of his hair, his eyebrows lowered in thoughtful concern.

Panic squeezed Olivia's chest. She'd almost got turned around twice. Finn could easily have gone in the wrong direction.

"We have to go look for him. I'll go with you. Finn should be here by now."

Scott sighed. "Well, we better go."

Olivia followed Scott along the sloping tunnel and back into the roar of the wind. The rain falling too fast made it impossible to see. Scott tripped and splashed into the knee-high water. Olivia followed closely behind, tripped over him, and fell in too.

Still sitting in the puddle, Scott shouted, "We must go back!"

Olivia thought about Finn. He'd protected her from a mob, supported her dreams, defended the Blue Kin, and accepted her. She'd be sad if she never saw him again, even if she didn't understand him

She had to find him, but didn't want to put Scott in danger. "You go back to Alan. I'll go on alone!" The wind flung her words away, and she wondered how much he had heard.

Scott heaved himself from the deep muddy puddle, climbed back onto the path, reached down, and yanked Olivia upright. He shook his head, but with his mouth to her ear, she heard, "You can't go alone!"

With a tight grip on her hand, Scott walked them around the puddle and started to run. Keeping up was difficult, but Olivia stayed on her feet, glad she was still in good shape. Running back through camp, she could see tents and huts swaying in the wind. A few feet of standing flood water covered the meadow. Even the higher parts were underwater.

They both slipped in the mud a few times but always steadied each other. They managed to make it to the beach path and almost to the beach when they saw Finn. Slightly off the trail, being held out of the water by a low bush. His eyes closed, and still. So still.

Scott leaped into action, letting go of Olivia's hand to wade through the water and get to Finn. He checked for breathing and slung Finn over his shoulder, and waded back.

Grasping Olivia's wet hand again, he pulled her in the direction of the ruins, shouting, "Come on, hurry!"

The wind was tossing things in the air. Sticks and other forest debris, small animals, and some tent poles in the meadow. Olivia kept on her feet under her, being nearly dragged by Scott.

She was starting to realize they would not have time to make it all the way back to the ruins when Scott yanked her into a group of trees barely past Main Camp. He led her down an opening into the smallest ruin she'd ever seen.

Like the others, it had bright mushrooms for lighting and woven paper walls with lots of pictures. Unlike other ruins, some effort had been made to flatten the floor with mud, and a couple sleep pads were laid out on the flattest part. "Where are we? Why did we stop here?"

Scott answered as he gently stretched Finn out onto the sleeping pad. "We don't have time to join the others. The storm is hitting now. We might be okay here. This ruin is on higher ground. Even if it floods a little, it's better than getting lost in the forest."

Olivia decided not to ask Scott any more questions. Talking was too much for her. She collapsed to the ground next to Finn. Was it just yesterday Puddles had warned them of the storm?

Exhaustion from the stressful day hit, and Olivia passed out next to Finn.

CHAPTER 16

Olivia

Exploring the disaster left behind after the storm, Olivia grinned. Actually, she decided, she felt truly cheerful. "This is great, really."

Dot frowned. "Except for the seven dead."

"Right," Olivia agreed. "Except for that, which is in, sad, but, don't you see? Everything is destroyed. This gives us a chance to start over, to do it properly this time."

Dot and Olivia splashed through the camp, the standing water nearly to their knees. "What are we going to start over with? Most of the tents and supplies are lost. We only have a small amount of food, everyone's new grass clothes are ruined, and the whole meadow is underwater."

Dot, usually so calm, sounded hopeless. However, Olivia felt different. This was her chance. To prove her leadership and build her community like she'd wanted. Instead of getting the mess of Main Camp.

"A while ago, Scott and I found the perfect place for a community. Well, technically, Finn was there too. Anyway, the ground is high there, and the forests have not been stripped of food. There is an amazing view, and we already named it Salt Cove. This storm was bad, but we saved all the tools, many of the tents, and all your small pottery. We'll start over, closer to the headland."

"Not everyone will view it the way you do. This is bad. It's upsetting people. They might leave and go to Blue Valley."

"Good. Anyone who doesn't want to be here should leave. That's been the problem from the start."

"You might have no one."

"I don't care. We tried to welcome a mix of the leftovers from the Main Camp, Jeff's crew, and Jeff-influenced newcomers. They can all leave. Then we can start the community we meant to."

Dot nodded, still carefully watching her feet, but with a stronger set to her shoulders. "Interesting. As long as you still have a plan, I'll follow you."

"I always have plans. Usually too many!" Olivia said with a grin.

Their spirits sagged a little when they found the remains of the cob house they'd been building. The base was sturdy and on a hill, so it was only damp instead of underwater. The roofless walls had not done as well, though, with whole chunks caved in or blown off.

"If we'd got the roof on, I think it would have been okay, even during the storm," said Dot. "This gives us hope for the future. The grass huts were flattened by the wind, but if we can make cob houses for everyone, then during the rainy season, we'll have a strong, safe village.

"Right," Olivia agreed. "First, we need to gather all the gear that can be salvaged and regroup. Then, we'll head toward the cove together. Spread the word for everyone to gather what they can to this spot, and we'll all sleep here tonight."

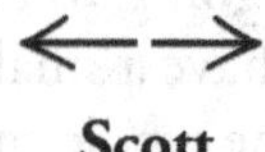

Scott

"Scott!" Alan waved Scott over with a welcoming smile. "What are you doing here?"

"I'm your partner today, to finish helping with salvage and a bit of foraging." Scott sauntered along the forest path near the meadow, enjoying a handful of berries. Olivia's enthusiasm was contagious, and he was happy again.

Scott popped one of the berries into Alan's mouth, making him laugh as he chewed and swallowed the offering, then said, "It's great, but you did the morning shift. I saw you."

"Maybe I volunteered for an afternoon shift."

"Why? You must be exhausted."

Scott fed one more berry to Alan and poured the rest into his own mouth, giving him time to reply. "Maybe I wanted to hang out with someone on the afternoon shift."

Alan's jaw dropped. "I've wondered how we kept getting paired. You've been volunteering for all my shifts this whole time, haven't you? Even if it means double work."

"Maybe." Scott smiled, an amused grin crinkling his eyes.

Alan pulled him into a tight hug and said, "I like spending time with you too."

Scott grabbed Alan's hand. "Let's go. I see pieces of a tent in that tree. Do you want to climb or catch?"

"Catch," said Alan. "You have stronger muscles for climbing."

"Sure do!"

"So, humble!" Alan laughed and pushed Scott toward the tree.

As Scott climbed, he asked, "So, any news from Jeff, is he taking a break from causing trouble while we regroup?"

Alan sighed, a long gusty sigh. "I doubt it. Did you know Jeff convinced people Olivia was just panicking about the storm and to stay in their tents? Then, he rushed to get to a group led to the ruins before the storm hit."

"What was he trying to accomplish?"

"I have no idea. I'm glad you were able to take some of them with you. The responsibility for this week's deaths fall squarely on Jeff."

Scott climbed a little higher toward part of the tent. Carefully balancing on a sturdy branch to pull it loose. "Have you heard anything useful being around Jeff?"

"He's already up to something again, but I don't know what. He won't talk around me anymore. We must have been seen together too much lately."

"So much for being Alan, the Double Agent." Scott yanked a tent pole out of the leaves and tossed it down.

Alan stood under him to catch it. "Ah, well. There are other things to discover."

The playful tone in Alan's voice drew Scott's eyes down, and he laughed, saying, "Stop looking up my skirt."

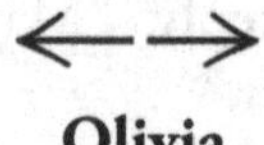

Olivia

Olivia yawned as she walked down the sloping entrance into the ruin, and Finn smiled at her. When he woke here yesterday, he was told he'd been knocked out for nearly a day. "How is salvage going?" he asked, leaning on one elbow in the makeshift bed.

"I had to slosh through the whole forest to get here. The water is not going away yet. Here or in the meadow. We've gathered everything useful and piled it around the community center. Enough tents still function that a temporary camp has been squished together on the unflooded high ground around the cob walls."

"I should be there, with everyone," said Finn, falling back onto the bed and staring at the mushrooms. The knot on his head throbbed and he wished for some of the meds in his bathroom at home on Earth.

"Maybe. You could still be too weak and it's safe here. We're nearly ready to leave soon, so you should rest until then."

Olivia's concern was nice, and with a slight shock, he wondered when he switched from thinking of her as an annoying attractive girl with a good idea, to a real friend. Or, maybe more than a friend. "Thank you. For saving me. Scott told me you refused to give up."

"You're welcome, but it was nothing." Olivia rummaged around in her bag. Eyes downcast.

Although her tone was offhand, her emotions whirled. He wished she'd look at him. "You could have died saving me."

"True."

"That's not nothing," he pointed out.

Olivia nodded and sat crossed-legged next to his pillow, laying out dry papers and a handful of charred burnt sticks for drawing.

Her thoughts became more focused, and she said, "Other new communities got to take only the people that wanted to go with them, and we got mostly undecided. At first, I didn't mind, but now, I don't think that was fair because we were not all like-minded. So, the new community at the cove will be better."

"Who is going to the new community?"

"It's invitation-only, or people can apply to join, and they must be voted in by more than half of the community."

"That would keep people like Jeff out."

"Yes, that is my hope as well." Olivia began to sketch, absorbed in her art. She started with a wide oval, placing groups of homes or larger buildings around the circle, with shared resources inside of it.

In the beginning, she planned out loud. Explaining to Finn as she marked off sections, describing her visions for a perfect lifestyle. Eventually, her voice trailed off. When she stopped talking, Finn sensed she was so intent on her project she might have forgotten he was still there.

He could tell he was getting sucked into her world again. Like the moment before the last big meeting. She'd painted such a perfect picture of the future that he'd wanted to live in that idea. Her hopeful enthusiasm was contagious, and her ideas and intense focus were charming.

He came back from his mental wanderings and saw the layout of the new community had his name written in the same cob house as Olivia.

Did she assume they would live together simply because she'd rescued him? Despite his thoughts, a moment before, had he given her any indication of romance? He remembered the dance on the beach, his hands on her waist. Okay, other than that, which was just how the salsa was danced. He had not even implied he'd be willing to date her, much less move in together.

Even though he acknowledged that the idea was not wholly unpleasant, he would have preferred her asking first. "Hey, what are you writing there," he asked to get her attention.

Olivia jumped, eyes wide like she wondered where she was. Then clutched the papers to her chest as she took in Finn glaring at her.

"Did you, uh, see my plans?"

"Yes." Finn poured all his annoyance into that one word.

Olivia groaned. "You were not supposed to see this one yet. Some are for much later."

He could feel Olivia's sincere embarrassment, but couldn't stop his anger once it started. "So, when were you going to tell me we're a couple?"

Olivia hesitated, her eyes distant and staring at the wall. Outwardly calm while her mixed emotions boiled under the surface, too complex even for his sixth sense to untangle.

The silence stretched, and Finn remembered why he didn't like Olivia. She was simply too infuriating to have a conversation with. She might as well be an alien for how little he understood her reasons or reactions.

Olivia jumped at the arrival of Scott. "Hey Finn, just coming to check on you. I brought some dinner. Hi, Olivia."

If Scott was aware of the stress in the room, he didn't show it. Laying out dishes and food on the other side of Finn, he asked, "Did you know it was Jeff who assured everyone there was no storm coming? He spread it around the camp to not bother to prepare and not to go to the ruins."

Olivia's inner turmoil flared into fury. "Easy to believe it's something he would do. We lost people and supplies to the storm. It's all his fault."

Finn shrugged. "Technically, that was Jeff's opinion, and it was only other people's choice to follow that opinion."

"Why are you defending him? You were only injured because he meddled. We could have all been safe before the storm hit."

Finn actually agreed with her. Why couldn't he stop himself from provoking her? The uncomfortable thought that maybe their communication problem was not all Olivia's fault flitted into his brain, but he squashed it. "It was my choice to go out in the storm and bring in the missing people."

"People that would not have been missing if not for Jeff!" Olivia stood, all her papers falling to the ground.

"Now it's your turn to storm out. Bye for now." Finn turned away from Olivia, catching sight of Scott's carefully blank expression.

Olivia's hurt and shock switched to determination. After a deep breath, she said, "Scott, I'm going to go help with the camp dinner now. When you have time, can you find someone to give a message to Jeff and his pal? Let them know they are not welcome to come with us to the new community. They can stay here in Main Camp or head to Blue Valley. Either way, they are no longer welcome as elders in my community."

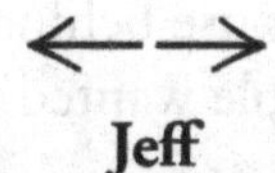

Jeff

"Banished? That lying child can't banish me!" Jeff started breathing heavily and collapsed onto the sleeping mat in the tent crowded with both their gear.

"Well, she's not banishing you from Main Camp. She's saying you can't go to her new camp. You'd still be here in Main Camp," said Dave.

"Living here, yeah, but not the leader. I need to take leadership from her to gain support from everyone."

Dave nodded.

"We've run out of time to finish our plans," said Jeff, "I've talked to most everyone about how Olivia is trying to silence me, and it could happen to them next. They are confused. It will be enough."

"Exactly. So, what do we do now?"

"Call a meeting. I'll be waiting at the entrance to that dumb house Olivia was trying to build. Have them gather there."

While Dave went to gather the remnants of this community, Jeff paced, planning out parts of his speech. The sun had mostly left when he made his way over to the cob house.

As soon as he took a stance in the best-lit spot, others began to arrive and settle between the two active cook fires.

The new group of ten dropped off today sat in the front, wide-eyed and nervous. Jeff tensed when he saw Olivia coming from the direction of the meadow and Scott lending an arm to a limping Finn as they made their way through the forest. Dot already sat at the back of the crowd with the other elders, a thoughtful look on her old, lined face.

So, all his enemies were here. It was time to begin.

"Hello, all. As you know, we are a broken community. Torn apart by a storm that our leader failed to prepare us for." He struck his palm with a fist, making eye contact with those in the group he knew were on his side.

"Even before the storm, our food was low and our chores unequal. The leader of this camp didn't even try to prevent lizards and bugs from infesting our pathetic homes. Instead, building this nice home for herself."

Jeff paused to gesture at the house behind him. All the best lies were built on truths, especially one's people wanted to hear.

"When I was the leader of a big company, I knew how to delegate and lead. I knew what I was doing. The companies I worked for made lots of money. Since I know what good leadership is, I can tell you that Olivia is not a good leader. I call for a leadership revote!"

He stepped forward slightly and swung his arms wide. Showmanship was always one of his best traits. Voices from the crowd backed him with a "yeah!" and "revote!"

Initially standing in the back of the crowd with her arms crossed, Olivia finally moved to stand near Jeff, facing the crowd.

She swallowed hard as all eyes swung her way, but said, "This man is no leader. He's been sabotaging the camp and is directly responsible for the people killed in the storm.

"Lies. How could I be responsible for a storm? Ridiculous. She's just trying to shift blame. I'm the only one here who can lead. I recommend myself as the new leader. By a raise of hands, who thinks I should lead the Main Camp?"

Dave, strategically placed near the front, raised his hand so everyone behind him could see it. The newcomers, unaware of the camp's history, reviewed their options of a belligerent teenager or one of Earth's well-known public figures. All raised their hands to vote for Jeff. This sparked all the people he'd been brainwashing to pitch in with their raised hands. It was more than half. He was in.

"You are no longer the phony leader. Hand over your leadership necklace." Jeff bottled up his triumphant gloating. That would come later. For now, he needed to appear calm and confident to this crowd of peons he was finally in charge of.

Olivia staggered forward, glancing at Dot, Finn, and Scott. None of them spoke in her defense, so she turned her attention back to Jeff, her angry glare changing into despair.

Wordlessly, Olivia lifted the necklace from her chest, leaving only her flower and vine shirt beneath. She passed the symbol of power over to Jeff and walked away from the group into the night.

CHAPTER 17

Olivia

Olivia lay on the beach with arms supporting her head, the cold sand smooth on her back. Staring into the sky, she traced the lines of unfamiliar star constellations.

Different planet - same story.

Every time she'd been excited about a new school, a fresh school year, or another class. Filled with hope. Sure, that this time would be different. She'd find a friend, a place to fit in, a sense of belonging.

She was wrong. Every time.

This place, so wild and unique. Surely this time would work. She'd even been put in charge, and yet. Different planet - same story.

She closed her eyes, blocking out the lights above and everything wrong with her.

It was always about two months in when people noticed she was wrong. Not like them. She could fake it for a while. Remember not to overshare, remember to look people in the eye, remember to act friendly and helpful. Blend in.

After a week or so, the fake started to show, or worse, she'd openly display when she was overwhelmed. Emotions taking over her words and actions. By two months in, she was alone and friendless. Like tonight.

She could blame Jeff, but maybe this was her fault. All the worst moments from the last weeks paraded through her head. Blaming the bathroom sign mix up on Scott's air-headedness. Not listening to Dot's warnings.

The worst was all the times she'd been trying to flirt with Finn and only made him angry. Her brief first boyfriend had been the same. Nonstop communication error until he broke up with her.

She was far away from her parents, her school, her comfortable home, her whole planet. The thought of Earth, the loss of it, was still a dull ache in her chest. She continually tried not to think about it. Now she'd lost everything here too. Her leadership role, her mentor, her only ever best friend, and Finn.

She groaned over again at the thought of him seeing their names together in a house. She'd been doodling, daydreaming about the future. He'd taken it wrong.

How could he not take it wrong when she was too scared to talk to him? She had refused to explain. Still her fault.

Olivia opened her eyes again, now filled with tears, feeling the usual loneliness return. With her entire view full of the bright spots above, it felt like she was floating in the sky with them. Adrift.

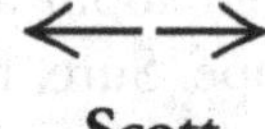

Scott

"Delivery," said Scott, approaching with Dot at his side.

Finn smiled at them. "What do you have for me?"

"This kindly old lady," said Scott, waving his hands up and down as if Dot was a prize on display.

Dot laughed. "Watch who you're calling old."

Scott grinned and shrugged before loping away on other errands.

"Morning Finn, would you like to join me on my walk? A new ruin pulling me."

"Sure." Finn set aside the rest of the green things he'd been chewing and followed Dot into the humid, wet jungle. Instead of paralleling the coast, she headed straight inland.

"So, what did you think about the meeting last night? Was the right choice made?"

"I misjudged Jeff. I thought Olivia was overreacting, but Jeff is dreadful. I was getting some strong emotions from him last night at the meeting, and he's meaner than I'd realized."

"I didn't need a sixth sense to know Jeff was trouble. I've been wary of him and Dave since they arrived. It's unfortunate they paired up."

"I think Olivia might have needed more support than we gave her."

"It's possible," agreed Dot.

The more inland they moved, the less standing water they encountered. Finn watched for edible plants as they walked, the camp was low on food, so anything he could bring back would help.

"I think I've been a bad friend. I talked Olivia into pursuing her utopia dream and taking over Main Camp for the Blue Kin. Then I sat back and watched her fail. Maybe leadership is a team sport."

"I know she would have appreciated your assistance," said Dot.

Hope swelled in Finn. "I'll do better next time! I promise!"

"Next time?" Dot asked.

"The community at the cove, the one she's planning." Finn blushed when he remembered the plans of their house together there.

Dot's forehead creased. "Is that still the plan?"

"I hope it's still the plan. That's where I want to live."

"She lost her leadership," pointed out Dot.

"She lost the leadership of the Main Camp. Who cares? She can still claim the high ground by the cove, we'll be even closer to the Blue Kin, and we can build her community there."

Dot didn't reply. She was circling a group of trees, searching for a way in. When she found it, she pushed two of the bending trunks apart and lifted a curtain of vines. "After you."

Finn stepped into the cave opening. These ruin entrances all appeared the same from the outside. A cave opening partly in the ground at half-human height, always surrounded by trees. He wondered again who created them. It could not be natural.

Heading down the tunnel, he came out to a regular-sized ruin, this one of the few where the roof had caved in. Sunlight streamed through the roof and lit the far wall. The fresh air dispersing the humid damp smell of other ruins he'd been in.

Picking his way through the piles of debris on the ground, he approached the wall. "These are Blue Kin symbols."

"Do you have the translator book?"

"Sure do!" Finn tapped his head. "Up here."

Dot laughed. "So, what does it say?"

"Beware the Biting Plant."

Dot shrugged. "Interesting. That warning is a little late. People have already died from getting bitten."

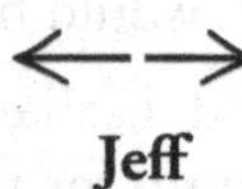

Jeff

Jeff was stumped. He was in charge of Main Camp. The Seat of Power. His shiny goal for the last several weeks, now tarnished by the duties it entailed. People keep wanting him to do things.

When he was a leader in the past, he had people do things for him. He wasn't required to make daily choices on how things were run. Or worse, share in the work.

Dave dispatched another runner and sat down beside him. "Are you okay?"

Jeff shook his head. "I'm in charge of a bedraggled little group of hippies and newcomers. I should have more power here, but I don't. Perhaps we should have tried to take over the Blue Valley group?"

"There was too much support for those leaders. As you know, you had to take over here first. Trust your instincts."

Jeff breathed a sigh of relief. His underling still believed in the plan, so he should too. Still though. "What's the next step, Dave? Maybe I've forgotten my original plan, but it seems to me that the groups have truly split up. Having leadership here doesn't give me the power I thought it would. I know more about power than anyone does. Believe me."

"Exactly. Remember, you still have access to all the newcomers for as long as they keep streaming in."

"Yeah, I'm just afraid."

"Afraid of what, sir?"

"Most people don't know this, but I grew up poor compared to the other rich families. The super-rich thing, it's an act started by my father and carried on by me. Trading on his powerful name. I'm scared because it now feels possible for me to become poor again, even as a leader. Before all the villages are settled, you and I, we must ensure we come out on top."

Dave nodded and put a reassuring hand on Jeff's shoulder. "It will be okay. I think your original plan is still sound. Take over Main Camp, and use the extra people here to create trade routes and become powerful that way."

"Oh, was that my idea? It's genius. Of course, it was my idea. Thanks for reminding me."

"Yes, sir.

"For this to work, we'll need outposts in both other villages and stopovers between them, plus an ongoing outpost here in Main Camp to continue swaying newcomers to our cause. We could get both villages so reliant on our trade routes that I'll be the richest and most powerful person on the planet. Yes! This is the plan forward."

Jeff burst out of his tent to start talking to people about how dumb an idea it was to build a tiny village far from other cities. Pointing out they should have followed the largest group and created a suburb. Like an outpost, or perhaps several outposts.

CHAPTER 18

Olivia

Olivia could not go back. She could not face all those people who believed lies about her. The warm weather invited outdoor sleeping. The mossy undergrowth at the forest tree line provided softer resting than the pad in her tent. For several days she slept in the cove near the Blue Kin. Avoiding the camp and the shuttle drops.

After weeks of constant talking and stress, the quiet of the waves and lizards was a welcome relief. Writing signs in the dirt was less stressful than finding words to say out loud. By the time Dot found Olivia, a calmness had settled over her mind.

"I'm glad to see you are okay. When you didn't return to camp, some of us were worried."

Olivia shrugged and nodded. "I'm fine."

"Will you listen to some friendly advice about leadership, love, and what is actually important in life?"

Olivia grinned. "I'll always listen to your advice."

"I've spent my life trying to understand where I fit in the world. People naturally gravitate to me as a leader. I made some of the same mistakes I've watched you make, and I understand. It's no fun to fail."

Olivia returned to her sad thoughts at this reminder of the mess she'd made. Worse, knowing that Dot had watched the chaos with a judgmental eye on her.

"You must become aware of places you went wrong," continued Dot, "so you are better equipped next time."

"Next time?"

"That's what Finn tells me. He says he's ready to follow you to the cove and build a community there."

Olivia's mind buzzed with new hope, new half-formed plans. She tried to push all that aside to focus on this moment with Dot.

"Leadership to help others is great, but leadership simply for power is the path to corruption. You landed somewhere in the middle of that in your last attempt. What I've learned works is what you wanted to start with. Build a community where everyone is equal, no head leader. I was an idealist in my youth, like you. Now I'm a realist. Still, possibilities for ideals exist, if applied carefully."

Olivia was not sure she totally understood, but she nodded.

"That's all I'll say for now about that. You'll learn with experience. Speaking of experience, you need a lot of work on how you talk to others, especially flirting."

Olivia blushed and stared across the water to the far horizon.

"You are still a bit young for this advice too, but everyone has to grow up fast on this planet. So, don't let little things get in the way of having a lifelong companion. Indifference is what you need to worry about, so as long as you are still arguing, he still cares about you."

"He does seem indifferent, most of the time. He ignored me for weeks unless he had to talk to me."

Dot chuckled. "Yes, but if he's been ignoring you on purpose, that's still an effort on his part."

She didn't fully follow Dot's logic, but it somehow gave her a little hope anyway.

"Finally, if you died in a year, what would you wish you had done in that year? If you died tomorrow, what would you wish you'd done today instead of sulking on this beach?"

Olivia had so many plans, dreams, and projects. She closed her eyes and imagined the community she wanted to build and live in. She imagined Finn there. With Scott and Dot.

Did she have the mental strength to try again? To give this another chance. Another fresh start. Maybe it would work better this time. Instead of the other fresh starts being with new people, these were people who already knew her and still planned to stay with her.

If she died in a year, she'd wish that she left a thriving community for future generations to enjoy.

If she died tomorrow, she'd wish she told Finn how she felt about him. If she really thought death was looming, she'd make sure she kissed him too. Would he want to kiss her? Did she have the daring to find out?

Dot cut into these thoughts with a pat on Olivia's back as she stood. "Whatever you are thinking so hard about, maybe you should stop thinking and start doing."

Olivia decided the old woman was right.

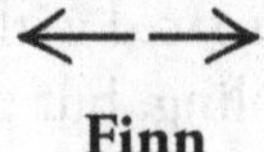

Finn

Finn had no idea he cared this much about Olivia. She'd been gone for days. She'd left her tent and all her gear, she hadn't taken any food, and she'd just been stripped of her community. He'd scolded himself multiple times that he had not gone after her. Now he didn't even know where to search.

He didn't have time to look, even if he knew where to start. Having Jeff as the leader was a nightmare. He was piling on extra busy work to those close to Olivia. It was retaliation, and Jeff enjoyed their frustration. Worse, he was going around spreading all kinds of conflicting plans, so the whole camp was confused.

Thinking of Jeff's terrible leadership made his thoughts circle back to Olivia. Again. She was not such a bad leader, now that he understood how much of a problem Jeff had been. He wished again he knew where Olivia was. They could gather their gear and a few friends and head to the cove she'd talked about.

Finn tossed aside the grass skirt he was trying to repair. He'd never been good at crafts, and being put in charge of clothing repair was torture. Glancing around the camp, he saw Olivia walking toward him.

His heart raced while his stomach tried out the skill of knot tying. She was back and seemed okay. Freshly washed and still dripping from an ocean swim, but her skirt was a ratty wreck and her hair a disheveled mess. She looked adorable.

As she got closer, he sensed resolve with a whiff of nervousness. Also, something else. "Hello, Finn. Can I speak with you, away from camp? Perhaps on a little hike, if you are willing?"

She was surprised when he said yes, and he felt guilty all over again for being so grouchy toward her since she became the leader.

She led, and he followed by her side. With all his senses spread wide, he soaked her in. Beads of water rolled down her shoulders and back, and he could smell the salt on her skin.

He sensed a new calm in her. More peaceful now and less conflicted. Where their swinging hands nearly touched, heat radiated from her skin.

After a moment's hesitation on his part, he grabbed her warm hand firmly, and her calm emotions soared with joy. They swung hands together all the way down the path. Smiling, but not speaking.

When she left the path, she let go of his hand with an apologetic twist to her lips. Leading them single file along a ledge to a cliff with a view of the ocean and the cove. The outline of Star Bay in the near distance.

"The view is beautiful," said Finn. "Too bad we can't make a camp here."

Olivia nodded. Staring across the bay to the headland, all that tree covered land stretching out into the ocean.

He would have been upset that she was not paying attention to him, but with his better sense of her emotions, he understood she was gathering her courage. He reclaimed her hand and asked, "What did you need to talk to me about away from camp?"

Olivia stared at their clasped hands, then glanced over at Finn and was caught in his eyes as if she could not look away. "Only this," she replied. She leaned in close, and when he didn't pull away, she rested her forehead on his.

The knots in Finn's stomach loosened, and he took in air, breathing her in. He tilted his head up and kissed her. She kissed him back and then pulled him close to hold him in a tight hug.

When he rested his head against her shoulder, she started mumbling into his hair."Sorry about the building plans."

Finn laughed. "No worries."

"I was daydreaming when I drew those plans, but I had an alternate plan for you, in a different drawing."

"Olivia, stop, it doesn't matter now. We should move forward together."

"Really?"

"Yes. It's easier to survive and build a new life with two rather than alone, and I want to build a life here. With you."

Olivia turned away to wipe a tear from her eyes and nodded. She didn't speak, but the emotions he got from her told him what she was too overwhelmed to say out loud. She took his hand this time, and they looked out over the inspiring scenery, thinking about the future. A future together.

CHAPTER 19

Finn

"How many are sick," asked Finn.

"Another today, and the two from yesterday," said Scott.

Only a couple days ago, he and Olivia were making plans to leave, but now?

They couldn't abandon the camp with people too unwell to care for themselves. Finn wondered briefly if the illness was contagious and if they should leave before it was too late.

All the sick people seemed okay, until they didn't. Collapsing where they stood, too weak to stand up. The people who had fallen yesterday were nearly paralyzed now. Surely it could only get worse from there.

Finn caught motion on the other side of the meadow and pointed it out to Scott. They watched together as a boy ran straight toward them, exhausted from the effort. He wore the tanned hide clothes of Blue Valley.

"Scott! I'm so glad I found you quickly. We have some kind of virus running through our population. It hit two days ago. We need help caring for the sick."

"We have our own ill here to tend. It's probably the same thing."

"How could it be the same sickness?" asked the boy. "No one from Blue Valley ever visits Main Camp."

Scott nodded. "True, but we send newcomers to you. Although, we haven't sent anyone that way for a week."

"Maybe it takes longer to spread?" asked Finn.

"Maybe," agreed Scott. "What does the doctor say? He went with you to Blue Valley."

"He was one of the first to get sick. It hit him hard, and he can't even talk anymore. He's frozen. All he can do is blink."

Scott sighed. "Let me take you to the Camp Leader. He should hear all of this."

Leading the boy to Jeff's tent on the far side of the meadow near the river they intercepted another message runner. A girl from the north village, Silver Tides.

Finn and Scott ushered them into Jeff's tent and turned to leave. Finn paused when Scott stopped. "Want to eavesdrop?"

"For sure," said Finn.

They crept to the back of the tent. Jeff's hut had flattened in the hurricane, and he was granted use of this borrowed tent. Sitting in the shadow cast by the setting sun, they tilted their ears toward the tarp and listened.

"The doctor went down on the first day and was too weak to help. Since then, a third of the town has become ill."

The other messenger spoke up. "We don't think it's contagious because it only hits people who have been here the longest. The newcomers from the last few weeks are completely fine. It must be something that builds in the body over time."

Jeff grunted acknowledgment of the comments and asked, "Do you suspect anything else?"

The boy added, "Our mayor has pointed out that not all the longest residents were sick, only those with a sixth sense. That was before he collapsed too."

"What?" asked Jeff. "Are you saying you don't have a leader in Blue Valley?"

"He's sick. It's chaos, getting worse each day. We need help. Since most of the original Elders stayed in Main Camp, we thought we'd ask for their help."

"Oh, you don't need that bunch of braindead old ladies. I'll go and lead in Blue Valley. I'll get everything running smoothly again."

"But sir, aren't you the leader here?" asked the Silver Tides runner. "Won't your own group need your help?"

"They'll be okay without me. When I'm the leader, with my good brain, I'll solve the sickness and maybe even make the aliens take us home, who knows."

Scott began to quietly move away from the tent, so Finn followed.

When they were out of hearing range, Finn laughed. "Well, more leadership just fell into Jeff's lap. He's outwardly calm, but giddy at leading two camps. From what I sensed, he's aiming for world domination."

Scott shook his head. "I knew there was something wrong with him."

"Let's go visit the sick. I'm ashamed to admit I've been avoiding them."

"Getting sick is scary, especially when we don't know what the sickness is. It's setting off all my anxiety. Still, if it's not contagious, you should go check on them if you want to. I have something I need to do."

When Finn arrived at the largest grass hut shelter, the three ill people stretched out on sleeping mats were being tended by Alan. Dribbling water into one boy's immobile mouth while holding a one-sided conversation.

"This little guy is Yoshi, he was born rather recently, and the only life he's ever known is riding on my shoulder."

Alan had not seen Finn arrive yet, so he carefully wiped the extra water from the bed-ridden patient and continued chatting.

"Ah, how did I find a newborn lizard, you might ask? It's simple, I took care of the mother, and she cared for the eggs. Lizard mothers here are so attentive to their eggs, not like most Earth lizards. I kept them safe and warm in a basket with a special lid, so I was there at the hatching. I had lots of pets on Earth, so I'm used to lizards."

Alan set the water aside and dragged a basket closer to himself. He pulled out another tiny creature.

"You are probably thinking now if you could one day have your own little lizard when you get better. In fact, you can! I've got a little guy ready who needs a friend as much as you do."

Alan patted the boy's bare shoulder and said, "I have to leave now, but I'll be back soon."

For the first time, watching Alan attentive and caring to potentially contagious sick people, Finn wondered if he'd misjudged him.

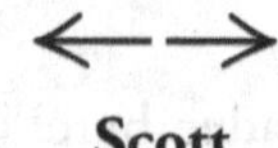

Scott

After parting with Finn near the new infirmary, Scott went straight to his not-so-secret-meeting-place with Alan. Luckily, it was still secret enough to give them some privacy.

He didn't have to wait long before Alan arrived, with a hesitant expression and some bad news.

"You are leaving for Blue Valley? Is this because Jeff is going? I thought you were done with him." Scott wanted to shout and cry all at the same time.

Alan reached out his arms to Scott, but dropped them when Scott didn't move closer for a hug. "I'm not following Jeff as one of his gang. I was staying in this community at first to support Jeff for a bit, and after because he blackmailed me. I always meant to move to the big village eventually."

"I thought you were staying here for me," said Scott.

"That was also a part of it."

"Then stay."

"I don't know if I could live this lifestyle. It's a little primitive," said Alan with a sad and amused smile. "Besides, I have plans. I want to open my own store, and I have the means to do it. You should come with me. We could run the store together."

"I can't leave Olivia right now. She has a truce with Finn for the moment, but she still needs me."

"You're a good friend. I can't fault you for that."

Scott's heart was breaking. "So, this is goodbye?"

Alan laughed. "We're still living on the same planet. Only a day's journey away from each other. Who knows, maybe Olivia won't always need you. Or, maybe I'll need you more."

Alan raised his arms again, and this time Scott fell into them.

"When are you leaving?"

"As soon as possible. I'm leaving in general because that is where I want to live. I'm leaving today because I've heard about the messengers. They need willing nurses in Blue Valley more than we need them here."

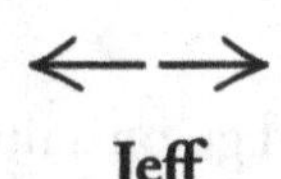

Jeff

Jeff smiled at the town he was the mayor of. All the doubts of the last week melted away as he strutted down the half-finished main street, remembering why he was the best.

He'd both convinced most of Main Camp to come with him and taken command of Blue Valley as a leader. He'd assured them it was temporary, but of course, he knew he would always hold this position.

As both the largest new settlement and the one that wanted to reinstate money, this was where he belonged.

"Dave!" snapped Jeff.

"Yes, sir?"

Jeff's mouth twisted into a smile at Dave's humble tone. Dave had come a long way from the angry cowboy he'd met when he arrived. Dave was so meek these days, so respectful. A good change. "Dave, organize these stupid fake-sick teenagers into their own camp, and when that's done, go around and let everyone I know saved them from chaos."

"Yes, sir."

As Dave veered away to carry out his orders, Jeff considered what he should do next to show his power. He could visit the ill, assured in the knowledge that he would not get sick. It seemed only those who had developed an extra sense were paying the price now.

Although, that sounded annoying. Instead, he decided to explore his new house. As mayor, he was allowed to stay in one of the only completely finished houses.

The house was almost like an Earth home. The wood used had a strange grain, and with no tools, it resembled a cross between a log cabin and a mud hut, but it was better than a dirt floor tent. Better than anyone else on this planet slept in, and that was all that mattered.

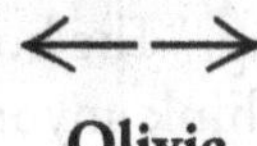

Olivia

Olivia sat too close to the fire, poking it with a stick. How could everything go so wrong in such a few days? It was all so clear standing on the ridge with Finn. Now, everything was uncertain.

Dot sat next to Olivia. Her eyes were glazed. Hopefully, she was not getting sick. "I think we should go on a little trip. Away from Main Camp," she said.

"We can't leave. Main Camp is empty except for the sick and the newest ten. We can't leave them alone."

"Of course we can. We are not responsible for everyone, and I think this is important. Another ruin is calling me, in the direction of Blue Valley."

"How could another ruin help us?" Olivia was in no mood for a hike, especially if she had to help carry a sick person back. With anyone able to fall ill at any moment, no one with a sixth sense strayed from the camp. She had never developed the extras, so eventually, she'd be the only caregiver to them all until they got better.

Scott appeared, a shadow emerging from shadows. "You need me?" he asked.

"I didn't call you," said Olivia.

"No, but I felt you needed me."

Dot sighed. "I think we do need you and Finn. I think we all need to head toward Blue Valley. Now."

Scott stood straighter. "Yes," he agreed. "I feel it too. We're needed there."

Leaving at first light meant the group arrived in time for dinner and the news of the first death from the sickness.

A heated discussion followed by anyone well enough to participate. Of what had caused both the new senses and the subsequent disease. Of the lists made trying to match locations visited, foods eaten, timelines of arrival, anything that could pinpoint what was causing the paralysis and death.

"Good grief," said Dot. "We're not getting anywhere with this discussion tonight. Let's sleep on it and gather again tomorrow."

An elderly man stood, saying, "The boy who died today fell into a coma first. Whatever this is, I don't think anyone will survive much longer."

Dot turned to their group and quietly said, "The ruin is still calling to me, but we can't go tonight. My intuition says we're here for a reason, so maybe we can help unravel this. In the meantime, let's visit the sick."

On arrival at the sick camp, Scott ran toward Alan, and they shared a tight hug.

"I had no idea they were so close," said Finn.

"I think it's been going on for a while," said Olivia. She saw Dot's smug smile and knew she must have known for longer than anyone.

Scott and Alan whispered a few more things to each other, then together, they jumped into caring for people.

CHAPTER 20

Olivia

"This is the largest ruin I've seen." Dot stood at a crossroads of tunnels, branching out around them. "Since we don't know what we're looking for, let's scatter and see what we find. Olivia and Finn, you go down that way. Scott and Alan can try that way. I'll keep going straight. Good luck, everyone, try not to get lost."

As the echoing steps drifted further away, Olivia held Finn's hand tighter. Alone, in the dark. Well, not quite alone, and not quite dark. She gazed at Finn. The angles of his face visible in the glow from the mushrooms along the ceiling edges.

She wondered who had planted these mushrooms and lined the walls with the paper-like texture. Why this civilization had not bothered with flat flooring, but had time to decorate all their dwellings with drawings.

"Do you think any of these people are left?" Finn asked. "Maybe deeper in the forest or somewhere on this planet?"

"If so, the aliens would have told us about them."

Finn nodded, but said, "The aliens were not very chatty. Maybe they forgot."

"They told us about the Blue Kin."

"True. I guess so. Actually, does that writing look Blue Kin to you?"

Olivia checked where Finn pointed above a low doorway. "It is! Written in the same flourishing style as in our guidebook. I recognize some of them, but you are better. What does it say?"

"The light is so dim here, it's hard to read, but I think it's directions. It says: Enter Here Story End."

"That hallway is so dark. It's pitch black in there."

"Maybe it's what we're looking for?" Finn took a step toward the dark entrance, pulling her with him.

"I don't like the dark," said Olivia.

"I thought you didn't like bright light?"

"I don't like that either."

Finn laughed. "It's okay. We'll go together."

Reassured, Olivia stepped with him, ducking low to access the long tunnel marked with the only words they'd been able to understand so far. The tunnel went longer than Olivia would have liked, and just when she was about to suggest they go back, they saw a lit room at the end. A circular room with a ceiling full of bright mushrooms. The walls were unusual, every inch covered in pictures with the Blue Kin writing underneath.

"Someone had time on their hands," said Olivia. "Can you understand it all? If it's language, do you know which direction to read it in?"

"This largest picture at the top by the door says start underneath it. I'll try reading vertically down from there. The drawings often go in rows."

Finn studied the wall, letting go of Olivia's hand to get close, squatting to read the low sections. After a few rows, Olivia asked, "Do you understand it?"

"I think so, at least a bit. It's a story. About a dying home world and evacuation. The next bit is tricky to understand, something about helping strangers, or strangers were helping them?"

"Could that mean the aliens, the ones that stole us?"

Finn shrugged and went silent again as he puzzled out the next section. In the quiet, Olivia tried to read some of the walls. Skipping over unfamiliar symbols, she made it around the room ahead of Finn, all the way back to the entrance. Symbols that stood out to her near the end of the writing included flower, kill, and death.

"Finn, this room is starting to freak me out."

Finn didn't seem to hear her. "They are so like us! They tried to form a single group, but failed and split up. They attacked the lizards, and a few of them died, so they came inland and tried to build here."

"Does it say what happened to them?"

"Yes, this part is easier to read. It summarizes that the group lived in peace, but fell ill as they started experimenting with eating plant life. Some of the plants were deadly immediately, but another plant waited. Uh oh, they called it the bite plant. Everyone eating its fruit acted strangely for many days, then fell ill, stopped moving, and died."

Finn frowned. "It says everyone. No one who ate the fruit survived. They realized much too late. The survivor wrote this tale and died alone." He pointed to the last drawing in the story.

A sketch of the Biting Nettle, with the symbol for death underneath it.

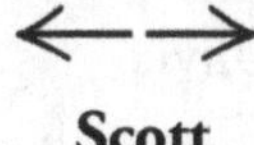

Scott

Scott tasted the sweet greens on Alan's breath as they kissed in a quiet corner of the dark hallways.

"Isn't this a spooky place to do this?" asked Scott.

Alan grinned, barely visible in the soft glow. "I think it's perfect. Romantic lighting with peace and quiet. What more could we want?"

"Somewhere a bunch of aliens didn't die would be good."

"How do you know they died here? We have not found any bodies."

"Well, I don't know, it feels disrespectful," said Scott.

"I'll give you that. Want to head back outside?"

"Yes, please." Scott leaned against Alan, relieved. "Although, this was nice."

Alan grinned again, grabbed Scott's hand, and started running down the tunnels. "Let's get you some fresh air."

"Are you sure this is the way back?"

"Well, I thought so, but this section is wrong." Alan started to backtrack, but halted when Scott didn't move.

"Look," whispered Scott, pointing at the walls in the rounded end of the hallway.

Like a madman had found crayons, the Biting Nettle plant was drawn over and over. Ceiling to the floor. Large and small. Stationary and in motion. Sometimes just the flowers, and sometimes just the fruit.

Scott pointed again, but this time to one specific section of the wall, "It's Blue Kin writing. It says death."

Alan ignored the wall while inspecting his friend with a worried frown. "Dude, you are sweating and a little droopy."

"I don't feel well," said Scott as he collapsed to the rough ground. Aware, but unable to rise, Scott grasped Alan's shoulders as he was pulled upright, then dragged to his feet with Alan's support.

"Help! HELP!" called Alan as they made progress at a slow forward motion.

Scott heard running feet. Olivia and Finn rounded the corner.

"What happened?" asked Olivia.

"He's sick, same as the others," replied Alan grimly.

Finn ran over to support Scott's other side, and between them, they dragged him toward the exit.

"We know what's wrong," said Finn. "It's the Biting Nettle. The fruit is a slow poison."

Alan pulled Scott into a better grip, asking, "How do you know? What is the cure?"

"It's what happened to the last civilization, the ones that made these tunnels. According to the owners of the ruins, it always ends in death. They never found a cure."

Scott finally spoke up, his breathing labored, "If I'm going to die, I need to tell you something. Put me down for a moment to rest."

"You are not going to die," said Alan, settling next to Scott. "We'll find a cure."

Scott leaned over and kissed Alan's cheek with a sad smile, and turned to Olivia. "If what Finn said is true, all three of us will die. You never ate the nettle fruit. I think a few others didn't either. If you find yourself alone, you need to know why we are here on this planet, so you don't do something stupid."

"What stupid thing would I do?" Olivia wrinkled her nose, but sat cross-legged in front of Scott, ready to learn whatever he needed to say.

"Don't try to attack the shuttle to go home," said Scott. "I should have stopped the last attempt, and I've carried that guilt with me since it happened. I know things. I know why we are on this planet."

"How?" asked Finn.

"I was in the first group. Actually, they told me I was the first captured. I was given the language guide and told the whole story."

"I can sense you are telling the truth. I've been so curious. And you've been keeping this from us the whole time. Tell us everything," said Alan.

"I don't have time to explain. I'm going numb. It's important to know that we can't go home. Earth is changing too quickly, and people won't survive. The aliens rescued us. Enough humans to keep the species alive, but they can't help everyone else on Earth, so we have to move forward."

Olivia took Scott's hands. "Why didn't you tell us sooner?"

"I decided to keep everyone focused on their own survival first and tell people later. If everyone was mourning their family, we could never have accomplished the progress we achieved."

Scott's head started to droop, so Alan tipped his friend toward his lap as a pillow. His breathing slowing, he held Alan's gaze. "I know I won't be able to talk soon, so, a couple more things. Olivia never had the berries, and Alan ate them late. If anyone can find a cure, it's you two, help each other."

Olivia met Alan's eyes over Scott's head. "We'll find a cure," Alan promised.

Scott nodded. "I know."

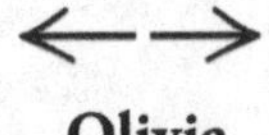

Olivia

Finn helped Alan settle Scott in the sick camp. He had not spoken again since the cave, mostly leaving his eyes shut. Although, his breathing had steadied for the moment.

Alan retrieved some water and started to drip it into Scott's mouth, saying, "So, what do we know."

Olivia also sat on the ground next to Scott, smoothing his hair.

Finn began to pace behind them. "I've been studying veterinarian books for years, and humans are mammals too. So, after a little thought, my guess is the plant poison slowly damages the brain. First, unlocking psychic ability, somehow, and then moving into the nervous system. Which causes paralysis leading to death."

"Are there antidotes? How do you make a cure for plant poison?"

"That's not something I've done a lot of research on. I think I remember either a plant is deadly or you can only treat the symptoms until the person heals. Either way, we don't have medications here."

Olivia wished she had something to add. She studied nature, but knew nothing about poison.

"We must find a cure!" shouted Alan.

Scott's eyes fluttered open and stared at them for a moment. His face twitched, but it was frozen along with the rest of his body.

Olivia's stomach churned when Scott's eyes closed again, and she put a hand on Alan's shoulder when he wiped away a tear.

"I'm sorry," Alan said. "I didn't mean to yell. I was just upset. Finn, let's see what else we can remember, and maybe we should go talk to Dot. She was headed toward the mayor's house. Finn?"

When Finn didn't reply, Olivia and Alan turned to find him passed out on the ground.

CHAPTER 21

Olivia

Olivia wiped tears from her eyes as she walked beside Alan. With both Scott and Finn unable to advise or stop them, they headed toward the beach, developing a wild plan Olivia admitted would probably get them killed.

Attack the shuttle.

"It's the only way," said Alan.

"You've said that three times." Olivia was not sure why Alan kept repeating that. Was he trying to reassure her or himself?

Alan ran a hand through his curls and sighed. "Sorry. I keep thinking of other ideas, and none will work. The last civilization didn't make it. They never found a cure. So, if we can find any chance of saving Scott, I have to take it."

"Agreed."

Having only gone this way once, Olivia estimated they had just enough time to get back to the beach before the shuttle landed. Passing through Main Camp, they checked for newcomers, and when they learned none had arrived yet today, they settled in the beach sand to wait.

Puddles came to sit by them, scratching a hello into the sand next to Olivia. "Do you know much of the language?" Olivia asked Alan.

"No, Scott is great at talking to them, though."

"Right? With Finn a close second. I've made some friends here, but I should have tried to learn the language faster." Olivia drew "Hello" and added a symbol for "Danger."

Puddle's orange antenna, previously forward and curious, now tilted backward as he glanced around the beach looking for the danger.

Trying to remember a few of the signs that matched the situation, she wrote, "Finn sickness danger help." She wished she could just tell him they were getting help from the aliens to save Finn, but she thought it got the point across.

Puddles read her message and wrote "Help" on his side of the sand, his head tilted and antennae swishing.

"Help," she wrote again, more clearly. Puddles scampered away. Olivia watched him communicate with the first lizard he ran into and the next, but her attention was drawn by the approaching shuttle.

Alan spoke as he watched it descend. "Are you ready?"

"Our plan is so basic, not much of a plan actually, but I guess it's all we have?"

"It will be enough," said Alan.

Olivia nodded, and they headed toward the shuttle, as if they were the usual welcoming party.

Eyeing the guns on top of the shuttle, Olivia put the first part of the plan in place. Sure that they turned off the automatic firing while people were on the ramp, she positioned herself facing away from the shuttle. Then started to slowly walk up the ramp backward as the newcomers stumbled down it. Sunblind, they were slow and cautious, stumbling into each other and her as they made their way down. When she was halfway to the top, Alan started the same process, walking backward a few steps in front of her.

When they arrived at the top, everyone else was at the bottom, but they were out of range for the overhead guns. The two guards wasted no time trying to spear them, but Alan flew into action. Kicking the tip of the spear away and getting in a solid punch before ducking under the next attempt to skewer him.

Alan kept one guard occupied, and Olivia followed the rest of the plan. Dodge and talk. As she kept her distance from the slower alien, she kept shouting, "I'm only delivering a message. I'm only delivering a message."

The guard almost got her, but Olivia ran swiftly to the far wall. She swirled around, ready to dance away from the next strike, but he'd stopped. At first, she thought her message had finally been accepted, but then saw the Blue Kin.

What seemed like every lizard in Star Bay was gathered. Either inside the room or on the ramp, with younger lizards around the outside of the shuttle. Storm had his mouth wrapped around the guard's ankle and was giving it a tiny shake.

The guard paled and asked, "You have a message?"

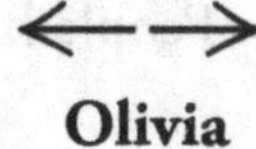

Olivia

Olivia watched Alan pace in front of the setting sun. "What is taking them so long?"

She didn't answer this rhetorical question. Staring at the entrance to the shuttle, willing help to come out of it. A few Blue Kin had stayed on the ramp, with a couple even standing in the entrance so they could not shut the door and leave.

A motion from inside caught her attention, followed by the giant lizards moving down the ramp, leading four blue-skinned aliens in outdoor clothes rather than their space jumpsuits.

Brown pants and boots, with a cream shirt and tan cloak. Three had spears, and the fourth wore a backpack similar to the packs given to each human castaway. A fifth smaller member became visible as they got closer. Her furry head had nervous twitching ears, and she was carrying a Blue Kin translation guide.

"Hello. So, I hear you two have had quite an interesting afternoon. Scaring our guards with your new allies," said the alien with the pack, clearly the leader of this landing party.

Olivia didn't like her tone or the implication they were causing trouble for no reason. "If your guard had listened to me, there would have been no need to scare them into hearing us."

The alien nodded and said, "My Earth name is River. I'm the ship's medic. This is Milky, the ship translator. The message I was given is that a few of you are sick and you want our aid?"

"More than a few of us, we're all dying. All of us!" Alan's outburst shocked River. She took a step back, almost stepping on Storm's tail. The Blue Kin glared at her and moved a couple feet away. Milky sat down and flipped open the guide to scratch in the dirt, translating for the Blue Kin.

"All of you sick?" River asked. "How?"

Olivia stepped forward. "We think it's related to a plant here. Their fruit tastes amazing, but at a cost. We think it's a slow poison, and we don't have a cure. We were hoping you do."

The medic frowned. "I don't have any knowledge of plant life here. It might take a long time to create an antidote."

"We don't have a long time. People have already died, and we're losing more each day."

"Well, let's go see this plant," said River.

She waved at them to lead the way, and everyone trooped along the beach path. River, Milky, their guards, Olivia, Alan, and several of the largest Blue Kin. Past the Main Camp, finally dry from the receding hurricane waters. Beyond the first try at a clay house, its roof still not finished. They arrived at the nettle Olivia had almost removed a dozen times.

Milky sat in the dirt again to translate, and the medic moved toward the plant.

"Don't get any closer. It bites," said Olivia. "The flowers have teeth to protect their berries. The bite is almost instantly deadly."

River sighed dramatically. "How am I supposed to inspect it from here? Guards, subdue this plant."

Each of the guards took aim and speared the flower through the middle, bending the stalk at an unnatural angle and pinning it to the ground. The plant quivered, laid bare.

Milky spoke for the first time, her squeaky voice also somehow soothing. "This being, Dusk, says he is the leader of his people. He says they know about this plant. He is asking if this is the plant making his friends sick?"

"Yes," said Olivia.

After a moment of watching the Blue Kin draw in the dirt, Milky spoke again. "Dusk says you are eating it wrong. This is a special plant in his tribe. It is The Giver. When a youth is old enough to start hunting, he is taken to these plants. The strongest hunters battle the plant so the new hunter can eat the berries and the leaves, giving the young hunter a new strength? That part is unclear."

Alan nodded. "Everyone who is sick developed a psychic power first."

"Yes, Dusk says, this is what happens, but it's important to eat the berries and the leaves. This is the lore of his people."

While they discussed, River had been examining the plant. "What leaves? This plant only has stalk, flowers, and berries."

Milky flipped through the book's pages, searching for better words. Finally, after a little more writing, she said, "Dusk says it's the little leaves. I can't make that any more precise."

Alan, standing by River, pointed to the plant cover around the base of the plant. "Do you think it could be those little leaves?"

Tufts of a small weedy plant grew around the stalks, among the exposed roots. It did not have any flowers, instead topped with tiny heart-shaped leaflets no larger than a thumbnail.

The translator conferred another moment and agreed, "Those are the correct plants. Dusk says you have to eat the tiny leaves of the plants, they usually have a youth eat all the berries followed by chewing all the leaves, and power arrives."

A weight lifted off of Olivia. There was a cure, an antidote to the poison. She simply had to take some of the leaves to Finn, but, "Many people are already in a coma, so they can't chew greens. How can they recover?"

The medic shrugged, "We'll save who we can."

"No!" The usually calm Alan stepped forward, causing the guards to move in closer to River. "We must save everyone. How do we get this plant into them?"

River tapped her fingers on her crossed arms and suggested, "We could blend it? With water?"

"Yes. Let's do that as soon as possible," said Olivia.

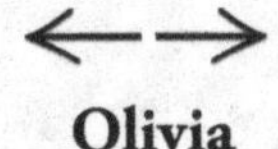

Olivia

Olivia watched the sick move slowly around the sick camp. Those who were not in a coma yet recovered quickly after chewing on the leaves. The rest of the sick, every human still standing, continuously dripped the blended plant water into the mouth of those too ill to move.

Alan sat cross-legged next to Scott, his back hunched, intent on dripping water from a rag straight into Scott's parted lips without losing any.

Olivia was doing the same for Finn, but neither of the boys showed any change in their condition. Olivia wanted to cry or ask Alan if he thought it was working, but instead reached for distraction. "Alan?"

He grunted in reply.

"I was wondering, you seem like such a nice guy. Why were you helping Jeff destroy the camp and sabotage me? I know you were directly involved in nearly all of it."

"I don't have a good excuse. At first, it was because I thought Jeff was cool. Later it was just fun and games. By the time it got too serious for me, Jeff had a hold over me. Somehow a boy died in Jeff's tent, and he told me I killed the boy."

"Jeff is the worst."

"He's a big liar. I know. I can sense lies now. At the time, he blackmailed me into helping him. I enlisted Scott to keep the worst of the dangerous stuff from happening, but I should have done more."

"About the boy, the one that died, I know you didn't kill him. I watched him get bit by a nettle." She hoped the information would ease his mind.

"Olivia! Look!" Alan's mixed joyful and urgent tone made Olivia drop her rag. When she lifted the rag from Finn's face, his eyes were open and wrinkled in a smile.

"We found a medicine, the Blue Kin and the aliens helped. We all found a way to cure you," said Olivia in a rush of words.

Finn coughed and said, "This is the fourth time you've saved me."

"Happy to help, Mr. Gloomy."

CHAPTER 22

Jeff

Jeff watched most of the humans on Aeymay. They were either bedridden, but healing, or assisting the sick. The crisis was over, with a successful ending. "This can only reflect well on me, believe me," said Jeff.

Dave, at his side, asked, "What, sir?"

"No matter how a problem is solved, the leader at the time gets all the credit," said Jeff with a wave of his hands, "and that's me."

"Is it?" asked Dave.

"Yeah! As the leader of the powerful Main Camp and prosperous Blue Valley. Now all I have to do is ensure everyone knows of my successes."

"Ah, your successes. I see."

"Everyone calls me a genius. I've had great successes. Next, we'll find a way to take over Silver Tides. I'll be Ruler of the Planet."

"Has a nice ring to it," said Dave.

One small part of Jeff still wanted to go home, to ruin his family's lives by taking back all his money, but Ruler of the Planet was a prize worth keeping.

Also, Jeff definitely enjoyed having a house and bed again. Given time he could build a good life here as the leader, with everyone to wait on him.

"Dave, you've been especially useful."

"Have I?"

"Yes, everything's been running smoothly."

"Do you even know what I do?" asked Dave.

Jeff paused before replying. Dave's tone was the same, but his words were wrong. More like the old Dave that he'd nearly forgotten had existed. "Uh, grunt work?" Jeff guessed.

"No. Not grunt work. After we arrived in Blue Valley, I've been coordinating the care of all the sick. Along with the usual running of the town, like food gathering and trash duties. During the last week, I've been arranging schedules for all the medications."

"Yes, as I said, you've been especially useful."

"Exactly. Useful. Because I am the leader."

"No. I am the leader."

"Wrong. It's me."

Jeff laughed. "You're a weak manager at best."

"Delusional. The Blue Valley residents have seen me everywhere, doing everything they need to get them through this crisis. They trust me."

Jeff went red, and his fists clenched.

Dave glared down at Jeff from his taller height and said, "No one cares about you."

Jeff gasped. Dave could not have known, but those were the words he'd heard from his father growing up. Unsettled, all he could say was, "but, but."

"The old mayor is dead, so the new vote is tomorrow, and I'll be voted in. I am the leader of Blue Valley, and you have nothing."

Jeff was the leader. It's what he'd been working toward all this time. Dave was only his servant. Yet, he could remember a time when he'd had to treat the man as a power-hungry equal. When had that changed? Seen in this new light, some of Dave's actions at Main Camp did seem odd.

Main Camp! With this one ray of hope left. Jeff grinned and pointed at Dave's chest. "You are wrong, old man. Even if you are the leader here, I'm not left with nothing. I'm still the leader of Main Camp."

"Main Camp was disbanded. Half are staying here, and the other half are creating a new settlement to the south. You have nothing, and no one cares about you."

"No. That can't be true."

"I'm still your friend, though. I can give you a place of power in the new government. If you don't run against me."

"You don't want me to even try to become Mayor?"

"If you run against me, you'll be an enemy. I can't appoint enemies to a place in the government I'm building. Which is sad. Because then you would really have nothing at all. You'll be poor again."

Jeff remembered telling Dave about being poor as a child. He could not go back to that.

"I'll make sure you are in charge of people. An easy job where you don't have to do any real work."

Jeff's anger battled with overwhelming disappointment. He had never worked a real job in his life. He would not know how to start now. If this was the only option left to him, he would accept it. His shoulders dropped. When Dave strode away, Jeff followed, dragging his feet.

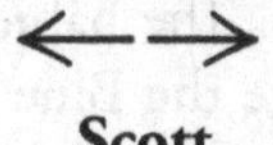

Scott

"Have you heard?" Alan twisted fingers through Scott's hair, laying on the ground next to the mat in the recovery hut.

Scott smiled at his friend's much lighter tone these days and asked, "Heard about what?"

"Dave is the new leader of Blue Valley. I had a chat with him this morning and learned some juicy gossip about this sixth sense."

"I didn't even know he had one."

"No one did. He's kept it secret this whole time. He said he was sorry for how things went in Main Camp and how he supported Jeff against me, but he was playing a long game to make sure Jeff never got to real power. His sense is that he knows what to say to influence people. He can't force them, but basically, he knows what to say to get people to do what he wants."

"A useful skill for a new politician."

"I guess so." Done with his tale, Alan snuggled close and settled his head on Scott's chest. "Are you still going with Olivia to the new settlement?"

"Yes. I need to help her get the Salt Cove community started. Are you still staying here in Blue Valley?"

"Yes, that is part of what I talked about with Dave. I'm going to build one of the main street shops."

Scott took Alan's hand, and they rested their eyes for a moment. "Alan?"

"Yes?"

"Thanks. For braving the shuttle to save me."

"I was just saving myself, really," said Alan. "I would have died too."

Scott laughed, knowing that was not why Alan had run off to assist with Olivia's wild idea. He wanted to say more, but he'd been so tired during this recovery. With Alan as a warm, comforting presence next to him, they drifted into a peaceful sleep.

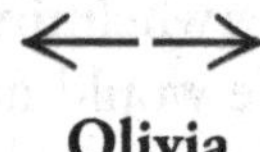

Olivia

Olivia watched the Blue Kin running around on the beach, chasing and feeding newly hatched lizards. The babies had burst out of the sand, and she remembered how attentive the Blue Kin had been to the sand before the hurricane, had these eggs weathered that awful storm?

"River!" Olivia called as the medic walked toward her shuttle, "Wait! If you have a moment."

River turned toward Olivia and seemed to hold in a sigh. "What do you need?"

"Can I ask you a few questions?"

"If you must." River sat next to Olivia in the sand, stretching out her long legs, and waited for Olivia to start.

"You use technology. Is there a reason we've been left with no tech? To live here like animals?" This was Olivia's burning question. The loss of tech had been hard on everyone, but especially her.

River snorted. "You've only had technology for a hundred of your years, and look at what you've done to your planet. Disgraceful. You've ruined it for all the current evolved life for who knows how long. If it ever recovers."

"What do you mean?"

"It's uninhabitable," said River, "or, it will be soon. Why did you think you were brought here?"

"No one knows!"

"We don't have time to explain it to everyone, but I was sure we told someone. I think it was a guy in the first group we dropped off, the one we gave a translation book to. He knows why you were all brought here as a rescue."

"He mentioned that, but a rescue? From what?"

"Recently, some humans have ruined the Earth for all the other humans. It will be inhospitable soon, and so a rescue was in order."

Olivia rolled her eyes. "Well, why capture people? Why not just announce it, so people can prepare and pack?"

"An announcement would not do. We cannot save everyone. You've overpopulated Earth, too many for that single planet to support. We have found you this planet. It's smaller and already has a native population, but they are willing to co-habitat with another species if you remain few and unwarlike."

"Humans tend toward warlike."

"True, but you'll have to grow out of that quickly. Maybe it will be a good learning experience."

River and Olivia watched for a moment as one of the baby Blue Kin skittered close to them and was chased back to the group by a babysitting youth.

"Oh, also, we've been wondering, why ten newcomers at a time?" asked Olivia.

"We could have hired a large ship to do it at once, but we didn't want to make a scene on Earth or overwhelm Aeymay with all the new people at once. Besides, Earth is already on our shuttle route. That's why we have assigned Earth names and know a couple of your languages."

"I still don't understand. Why did you mostly take teenagers?"

"We didn't 'take' anyone, we rescued you, but we didn't want to disrupt any settled lives. So, we focused on the young. It would not be as hard for you, similar to other baby animals separating from their parents."

"You don't seem to like us much. Why not just let the humans die?"

"You are full of questions. The alien council passed laws long ago, agreeing to protect all sentient life. Even if you are barely more than animals, and you did bring this on yourselves, you still fall into the category worthy of preservation. My family business was hired to carry out the council's wishes of relocation. We were given a budget for transport and your supplies."

Olivia remembered the flimsy tent, thin sleeping mat, and tasteless ration bars. Either the council didn't actually care much about them, or someone had bought junk and pocketed the extra money.

"One last question. How many people are being rescued? How many will we have in the end?"

"It was calculated that about five hundred human castaways would be enough to ensure genetic diversity."

Olivia narrowed her eyes, saying, "Strange word choice: castaway."

"That's what you are," said River. "Survivors of the human race."

"What if we didn't want saving? What if we want to go back?"

"Impossible. Your planet's climate is too unstable and no one will survive."

At sunset, the Blue Kin herded their young towards the southern cove for the night. Olivia and River sat in peaceful silence for a moment. The alien said, "You know, I always wondered what happened to the past castaways here. The stories of them were from before my time, but it was always odd they simply vanished. I'm glad you will survive."

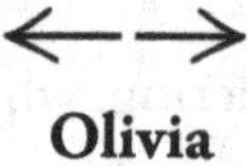

Olivia

Olivia sat quietly next to Finn, listening to everyone chat. After the overwhelming events since her capture, or rescue, this was the first time she felt okay.

Getting an understanding of the whys of everything from River. Knowing Finn was safe and they would be together. It helped. Sketching the plans to build their little community kept her hands busy and it helped too.

She came back to the conversation as Alan said, "I still have my power too. I guess they are permanent, even after the cure?"

Scott nodded. "Some of the newcomers are hearing what happened with the Biting Nettle, and then going out in the forest to battle it and gain their own power. It's become a bit of a ritual, rather like the Blue Kin have."

Finn grabbed Olivia's knee and jiggled it. "So, are you ready for your power? Shall we take you into the forest and fight a monster, so you can eat some delicious berries that disintegrate parts of your brain?"

Olivia snorted and shook her head. "I'm fine as I am. I like my brain."

"Me too," said Finn and kissed her cheek. Olivia smiled and returned to her drawing.

"So," said Alan, "You are all heading out tomorrow?"

"Yep. In the morning," agreed Finn.

"Blue Valley will miss you," Alan said to the group, but mostly stared at Scott.

Finn jumped into the silence. "You'll have plenty to do here. Scott tells me you're opening a pet store?"

"The first pet store in the new world. I'm funding it with all the gold I've found."

"Gold?" shouted Finn.

"I have not wanted to start a frenzy, so I've kept quiet, but every time I find an area with gold, I've been marking it with a pile of rocks in a specific design. My metal detector is finally dead, but it worked long enough to make me money for this fresh start in Blue Valley. Dave is going to mold the gold into coins and pay me back in labor and food credits. He's actually kind of a good guy."

Olivia snorted quietly. She may have forgiven Alan completely, but she wished the aliens had taken Jeff and Dave back with them. When Olivia asked if the troublemakers could be returned to Earth, River had refused to take them.

If they must be on the same planet, at least they would be in the town furthest from her new coastal village.

Actually, on reflection, she was glad of everything that had happened in her last attempt as the leader. She had learned a lot about what not to do. She wouldn't choose to live it over again, but since she'd made it through to the other side, she could appreciate the silver linings.

In taking away her leadership, Jeff had shown her that she didn't want to lead anyway. She didn't want to be in charge. Olivia simply wanted to build something wonderful.

Jeff had saved her from a stressful future with lots of people in it. She would not have to deal with complaints, meetings, and enforcing rules or jobs. Olivia could live a less stressful life in the path Jeff had pushed her onto. One where she and her neighbors were more like family, all equals.

She reached out and placed her hand over Finn's. He flipped his hand over and intertwined their fingers as he continued to chat with the other boys.

It was impossible to draw with only one hand, so she set aside her papers and listened again to their conversation.

"What do you think we'll find deeper into the forest or over the ocean? Humans have a whole new world to explore," said Scott.

Olivia frowned. "Aren't you afraid we'll multiply and ruin this planet too?"

"Hopefully not," said Alan.

"It's kind of what humans do." Olivia sighed and twisted the grass of her skirt. Feeling the usual sad hurt about the destruction of Earth by humans.

"I don't think we have to accept those old ways," said Alan. "I think we have the chance to do something completely different here. We can change stereotypes about people and about land use."

"True," agreed Olivia. "I've acknowledged that I can't control others, but the old people will die off soon. Our generation can all be good leaders and examples for change. We can make this a lovely place for future generations."

Alan smiled at her, "I applaud the values of your new primitive community. In the meantime, I'm going to work to change opinions here in this town too. Everything is connected, so it's better to be part of the web than outside of it."

Finn nodded at Alan and Scott, then he smiled at Olivia. "I'm excited to build this new life together."

EPILOGUE

Sarah

Sarah strolled down the dusty sidewalk, admiring the interesting structures along what she'd been told was the main street. Some were still in the building process, but most were finished.

As the last off today's shuttle, she was told she was the last Earthling to arrive at Aeymay. In her choice of locations to live, she was offered a tribe to the south, a small bartering community to the north, or this inland civilization.

A real town sounded like the best option. This town was still too small for her as a city girl, but she could see how it would grow in the future, and the people were friendly.

Sarah had been an international student picked up with a group from Japan at the school she attended. Her wispy long red hair stood out in the island country, but here, with an odd assortment of Earth clothing and natural wear and a mix of people from all over the world, no one stood out.

Eagerly determined to visit every shop before heading back to her temporary tent for the night, she wove in and out of stores. Both built and half-built.

On exiting a lighting shop, she heard a man down the street yelling toward the mayor's office about being put in charge of the trash department. He was easily the most oddly dressed she'd seen, wearing big orange leaves like a hat, and being kept out by guards.

To escape the madman's rantings, she popped into the next doorway, and to her delight, discovered it was a pet shop. She'd interrupted the two boys behind the counter as they shared a brief kiss.

The curly-haired boy said, "I'm Alan, and this is Scott. You must be from the last drop. How do you like Blue Valley so far?"

"It's perfect," said Sarah. "The whole town has a fresh, hopeful vibe. It all feels like a new adventure!"

If you enjoyed this book please leave a review,
and share with friends!

Follow me on Amazon to find out about upcoming books,
and visit me at www.starrgreeninfo.com

BIO

Starr Green is an autistic creative thinker, and when not writing, is pulled in all directions as a mom and administrative assistant. She lives in the Pacific Northwest and has a degree specializing in Environmental Communication from Oregon State University. As a teen, she was delighted by all the worlds she discovered in the local library. Her debut novel Castaway Strangers is the first of her many fantasy books with female autistic characters. Find out more at: www.starrgreeninfo.com

Sneak Peek!

Want more books with an autisic female lead?

Read the exciting first installment of Piper's journey in:

Sailing in the Sky

Wave Sweeper Trilogy Book 1

by Starr Green

An autistic runaway joins modern gods in a dangerous

search for missing humans while falling in love.

Enjoy this start of Chapter One...

Piper stepped on top of the sand, trying not to kick any into her sneakers. Normally she'd take her shoes off at the beach, but today time was limited. She was only here to say goodbye to this stretch of coastline.

The beach contained a short path bordered by clumps of palm trees, with rooftops of beach houses in the near distance. The sandy trail started at the end of a boardwalk connected to two low fishing piers, wooden sidewalks stretching out into the water just above the high tide line.

A short distance into the sand was as far as she wanted to go today. Reaching a specific palm tree, she pressed her hand against the bark in a silent farewell. Mentally offering it thanks for sharing its shade all these years. At only a two-minute stroll from her home, the tiny beach became the one place she was allowed to go alone. It was her approved daily exercise, and it was being taken from her.

"Hello? Hello? Help!" A voice broke through her thoughts. It sounded young, or at least childish. High-pitched and, even in panic, adorable.

Piper scanned the area and could see no one. "Where are you?"

"Here! Here!" Huge eyes attached to an impossibly large head emerged from the water and peeked over the edge of one of the low wooden piers. "Help!" Piper could not recognize the creature with its large solid black eyes protruding on each side of a massive scaled head, they shifted forward to focus on her.

The creature with the eyes must be the owner of the voice, but she had never heard of a sea creature that could talk. She moved forward cautiously, retrieving her suitcase from the boardwalk on the way. Taking deep breaths to calm her fast-beating heart.

Piper had read library books full of stories of magic and magical beings, but surely that was all made-up fairy tales? She had never believed them. Now belief was unnecessary, the evidence was rising out of the water in front of her.

As she got closer, she could see the eyes were placed under enormous rounded ears of a narrow head with a wide jaw and small rows of teeth. Two long snake fangs gleamed white in front. Purple-tinted iridescent scales in teal and emerald lined the head and the humps sticking up out of the water. A dragon. Still, she could not help but ask, "What are you?"

"You talk!"

It was a speaking sea creature, why was it surprised at her speech? "Of course, I talk. I'm human."

"I never see you talking."

"Have we met?" Piper was certain she'd remember encountering a dragon.

"No. I have watched you for many days now."

"Why?" Unsettled, Piper stopped her forward motion. The creature had been calling for help, but was now simply conversing in a happy bubbly tone. Perhaps calling out to lure her over here was a trap. Would the dragon eat her? Probably not, she decided.

"Ah. Not watching. Maybe noticing. I swim here lots and you walk here lots."

"I do, every day."

She wondered if the dragon noticed how she refused to talk to people if possible. Maybe it had been watching the times she saw a stranger coming on the path and would run back the other way and hide in the trees simply to avoid having to say hello to people she didn't know.

Maybe the dragon knew she would not want to talk and so had pretended a problem existed simply to get her attention. "You called for help?"

"Oh, yes. I am stuck. See?" The dragon's midsection rose out of the water, the webbed fins along its back tangled in a thin fishing net. "Can you remove it?"

Evidence of how large the dragon was did not settle Piper's mind. Instead of agreeing, she boldly asked, "Are you planning to eat me?"

"No, no, yuk. I eat only fish."

"What are all those teeth for?"

Instead of answering, the dragon considered for a moment. "You help me and I'll give you a gift." It raised its netted midsection again and wiggled it toward her.

Piper was not sure she wanted a magical gift. Fairy tales often implied there were good and bad sides to accepting such offerings.

However, it was not in her nature to stand by and refuse help to a creature in need, and she would always wonder what happened to the dragon if she said no.

She took one step closer to inspect the netting. It was spiderweb-fine, but looked strong. If the net was pulled too hard, it might rip the delicate webbing of the fin along the dragon's back. She would have to untangle each section. "Come closer," Piper said, kneeling on the pier and reaching out over the water.

The first touch of her hand to the dragon's scales surprised her. She expected them to be smooth and wet, but instead, they were coated with thick slime. Piper pulled away. Her fingers splayed as she considered how to get the slime off.

She paused, remembering that she was trying to be braver about touching sticky things. She already had the slime on her hands, so might as well continue even if it was unpleasant. Bracing herself to touch the slime again, she bent to the work.

Removing the net proved possible, but was difficult with her slippery cold fingers. How could a clever dragon get so tangled? She must not have been paying attention. Wait, she? Or he? "Are you a boy or a girl?"

"What do you mean?"

"Like, I am a girl."

"I am not human."

"True," Piper felt that way too sometimes, "but I mean… surely you know of… dolphins out in the water, and some are male and some are female."

"I am not a dolphin either." Its neck scales rippled. Raising and resettling.

"Yeah, but I mean, what should I call you, he or she?"

"Call me by my name. Fia."

"Will do." Piper was often confused in a conversation or misunderstood the point. It was odd being the one to explain a topic to someone else confused by a conversation. It was like talking to herself.

The dragon was not too tangled at first, but the more Piper removed, the more the dragon squirmed and became ensnared. "Can you stop moving?" Fia obligingly held still and was soon free. It was almost too easy after what had seemed intentional prolonging.

"You are all set." Piper washed the goo off her hands in the seawater and dried them on the edge of her jacket. "Bye."

"Wait, don't leave yet. Talk more."

Piper paused, her initial fear mixed with curiosity had been replaced with marvel at being so near Fia. Besides, when was the next chance she could talk to a dragon? "I need to catch a bus, but I probably have a little time left." Piper set down the suitcase again and sat on it.

"You never had a bag before on the beach, are you leaving? Where are you going?"

"I'm not sure. Just… away." Piper's gaze drifted over each of the visible scales, nearly losing herself in the examination of the colors fading into each other.

"If you leave, will I ever see you again here?"

"Probably not. I can't come back." Although why the dragon would need to see her again, she had no idea.

"You like it here," said Fia.

"Yes, I love it here, but I must leave as soon as possible." Piper's stomach dropped again at the thought. It had been doing it all day.

"Do you want me to help you leave? You could ride on my back."

"No thanks, you're slimy."

"What if I had another way?" Fia's not entirely unpleasant breath huffed out in what Piper thought might be a laugh.

☘☘☘

Read more in:

<h1 style="text-align:center">Sailing in the Sky</h1>

Wave Sweeper Trilogy Book 1

by *Starr Green*